# DUBLIN NOIR

# DUBLIN NOIR

## THE CELTIC TIGER *vs.* THE UGLY AMERICAN

### EDITED BY KEN BRUEN

AKASHIC BOOKS
NEW YORK

## Also in the Akashic Noir Series:

*D.C. Noir*, edited by George Pelecanos

*Brooklyn Noir*, edited by Tim McLoughlin

*Brooklyn Noir 2: The Classics*, edited by Tim McLoughlin

*Chicago Noir*, edited by Neal Pollack

*San Francisco Noir*, edited by Peter Maravelis

## Forthcoming:

*Manhattan Noir*, edited by Lawrence Block

*Baltimore Noir*, edited by Laura Lippman

*Twin Cities Noir*, edited by Julie Schaper & Steven Horwitz

*Los Angeles Noir*, edited by Denise Hamilton

*London Noir*, edited by Cathi Unsworth

*Havana Noir*, edited by Achy Obejas

*Wall Street Noir*, edited by Peter Spiegelman

*Miami Noir*, edited by Les Standiford

*Bronx Noir*, edited by S.J. Rozan

*Lone Star Noir*, edited by Edward Nawotka

Series concept by Tim McLoughlin and Johnny Temple

Published by Akashic Books
©2006 Akashic Books

Dublin map by Sohrab Habibion
Editorial assistance: Emmet Henry and Chris Gough

ISBN-13: 978-1-888451-92-4
ISBN-10: 1-888451-92-0
Library of Congress Control Number: 2005925466
All rights reserved

First printing
Printed in Canada

Akashic Books
PO Box 1456
New York, NY 10009
Akashic7@aol.com
www.akashicbooks.com

# TABLE OF CONTENTS

## PART IV: NEW WORLD NOIR

# INTRODUCTION

**B**rooklyn Noir was a huge success, set a bunch of authors to write about one place, simple and highly effective.

Now in Akashic Books' "noir" pipeline are Manhattan, Baltimore, Miami, Los Angeles, Havana, London . . . and that's just the beginning. Here is *Dublin Noir*.

At first, it was straightforward—Dublin authors to write on their city . . . Then we turned the concept on its head, as you do in noir. The Irish are fascinated by how we appear to the world, so let's have a look, we thought, at how this city appears from the outside. In addition to a couple of us locals, let's take a cross section of the very best of today's crime writers from America, as well as Britain, Europe, and Canada—the successful ones, the new blood, and those between. We knew we'd get a lot of Yeats and Ulysses, but what else . . . ?

The challenge we posed to the authors we invited to join this collection was simple: Show us *your* Dublin, and show it noir.

Tourists booking holidays in Ireland inevitably do Dublin first and seem to always end up in Temple Bar, our very own Times Square—replete with the squalor, the drugs, the homeless, and the wandering psychos. Two years ago, Pat Boran, the legendary director of the Dublin Arts Festival, invited me to do a reading in Temple Bar. During my gig, a woman up and died. It added to my already noir rep and has certainly given me pause about returning there. Temple Bar, naturally, features in many of the stories, and the authors certainly capture the noir element. The Tourist Board, not fond of me in the best of times, has responded with a bounty on my head. I take that, I think, as flattery.

Ireland's alleged surging economy—the "Celtic Tiger"—has thrust Dublin onto the world stage, though here the city's not exactly seen through rose-tinted glasses. Black Irish humor shines in all the stories, as if instinctively the writers knew: You want it Dublin, then you want it funny as sin, dark as the smile on Joyce's face when he found he was on the index of banned books. To be Irish is to dance on the Titanic; laughter is indeed the best revenge, it's our way of evening the score.

You won't find many leprechauns or bodhrans here—and not one *top o' the mornin'*. "The Quiet Man" has gone dark, and with a vengeance. If nothing else, this collection will kill stone-dead the Irish caricature of shite talk and blarney. In the days of Brit occupation, to be outside Dublin was to be outside the pale. This collection is so far from that parameter, you can't even see the boundary.

Like Irish logic at its most convoluted, this volume offers up a story that moves from Budapest to Dublin written by a Texan. In another, Ray Banks, from Manchester, England, presents a vision of Dublin as fierce as any Celt's. One of the collection's tastiest moments comes when Peter Spiegelman's femme fatale tells his protagonist, "Yer pretty feckin' Irish for a New York Jew, Jimmy—you'll fit right in in Dublin." The one guarantee from every story in this book is a skewed perspective on this most volatile of locales.

We set John Rickards, an impossibly young writer, loose in Dublin—a British mindset carried in an American style—to see what would happen. James O. Born, a Miami homicide detective, gives us a *radical* (to put it mildly) take on the Irish tourist industry. Laura Lippman and Sarah Weinman masterfully bust up our sketchy designs on an all-guy lineup.

And how could we do this without the culchie take? . . . So we have the Galway view on Dublin, always going to be contentious. If nothing else, we knew it would make Nora Barnacle smile.

The dictum, *Only connect,* was brought home to me in Las Vegas. James Crumley, renowned mystery writer, asked, "Wouldn't it be something to connect all these different countries, have them united in crime?"

Dublin, locus of so many literary legends, seemed a fine place to connect some dots. Enjoy.

*Ken Bruen*
*Galway, Ireland*
*January 2006*

# PART I

## THE INSIDE JOB

# TAKING ON PJ

BY EOIN COLFER

There were three words that Christy didn't want to hear.

"He sent PJ," said Little Mike, pulling his head in the apartment window.

Those were the three words.

"He's on the way up."

Those five weren't great either.

"Shit," swore Christy. "One bloody can of Fanta. One can."

Little Mike shrugged. After the high wind, his black hair looked drawn on with a crayon. "It's the principle with Warren. Steal a little, steal a lot. He don't care, Christy."

Christy chewed on a nail. "I was waitin' and I was thirsty and the fridge was right there. Hummin'. So one bloody can."

Little Mike tried to flatten his hair. "He does that. It's like a test. Leave you waiting in his shop, surround you with product, see if you can keep your paws off. Go against your nature. Did you ever hear the story about the fox and the scorpion?"

Christy threw whatever was handy at Little Mike. "Fuck off with your scorpion. The whole world knows that story. Every time the shit hits the fan, some fucking wise man trots out the fox and the bloody scorpion. I am up to here with those two, honest to Jaysus."

Mike rubbed his crown, where the Fanta can had clipped him. "I was only sayin'," he said, sulky now.

Christy folded immediately. He had enough enemies, and one of them was on his way up the eight flights.

"Sorry, brother," he said, knuckling the spot where the can struck. "I've a bad case of the freaks. This fucker is an animal. Did you hear what he did to Father Hillary?"

"The Paschal candle thing?"

Christy shuddered. "Jesus Christ. You know how big those things are? Some of 'em have studs too."

"Hillary was a nice old eejit. I mean, what did he do?"

"Wouldn't split the Sunday take, I heard. Sixty-forty, Warren says. Hillary says go to hell, so PJ did the job with the candle." Christy was pacing now. "A priest. A bloody priest. What will he do to me?"

Little Mike wasn't the best with rhetorical questions. "Jesus, now you're asking. I'd say he'll break a few things, make an example of you. Zero tolerance, as he's always saying."

"That, and do you like the car's new bulletproof windows? I mean, they look the very fucking same. What's to like about them?"

Little Mike cleared his throat. "To get back to PJ. Please God, he'll stay clear of your mickey. Some of these enforcers are a bit quare, you know. They do stuff to you. I've heard stories about PJ. Worse than the Paschal candle."

Christy sank into the sofa, wiping his mouth over and over. "Maybe if I explain . . ."

"What? Like, talk to PJ?"

"I'll tell him. I was there to turn over the bag money. I was just waiting for Mister Warren, and I forgot where I was. Thought I was in a normal shop. Just robbed the can like I generally would. So here's the euro, no harm done."

Little Mike hadn't the strength to laugh. "I hope you lie better than you tell the truth. Jesus, that was shite. He'll ride the both of us with the leg of the table if you tell him that. I think we better just go."

Christy had always been the brains of the duo. "Go where? We're on the top bloody floor. The lift's knackered. So unless there's a helio-bloody-copter on the roof, the only way is down."

Out in the hall, the banisters clanged and vibrated. PJ was battering a tattoo. Jungle drums. Every door in the block would be locked before the rattle faded.

"We're shagged," breathed Christy, the mascara running down his cheeks.

"That makeup looks fuckin' stupid now," said Little Mike. "You look like a bloody panda or something."

Christy found a nugget of pride somewhere. "This is cool, right. Yer man from Manic Street Preachers wears this, and yer man from Busted."

"Mebbe. But they don't go streaking it by bawling all over their faces, do they?"

Christy's panda eyes squinted. "Well, PJ is coming up the stairs with God knows what under his coat. Any rock star you care to mention would shit himself."

"Not Lemmy," said Little Mike defensively.

"Yes, fucking Lemmy. And Bon Scott."

Little Mike crossed himself. "Ah, now. That's a step too far. Don't talk about Bon."

Christy could actually hear footsteps on the stairs. Slow and deliberate. PJ was giving him time to jump out the window. *Focus*, he told himself. *Think about what's actually happening.*

"Shut up, Little Mike. I need to think about what's actually happening, not Bon Scott."

"That was always your trouble," said Mike with a few sage nods. "Drifting off. Remember when Miss Doyle asked you

Colombia's main export and you said forty-eight? Sure, that was the day before."

A soft idea began firming up in Christy's head. "What if we took PJ on?"

"Coffee," said Mike. "Any eejit knows that. But it wasn't that you were stupid, you just never nev . . ." He stuttered to a halt. "Who? Take what on? Do what?"

Christy jumped to his feet, grabbing his friend by the shoulders, trying to keep the idea going. "Look, PJ's coming in that door any second. He's going to break a few bones, and probably do a few deviant things in the riding department. You're not walking out either. You know what he's like."

A tear appeared in the corner of Mike's eye. "You and yer fuckin' Fanta."

"I know. Don't I know. So why don't we have a go? There are two of us."

Little Mike realized that his friend was actually serious. "Two of us? Father Hillary had God Almighty helping out, and look where it got him."

"I know. But we're a team. For years, since primary. Batman and Robin."

"Robin got killed," said Mike.

Christy was shocked. "He did not, did he? Jesus, I didn't hear about that."

"Yeah. It was a big shock. The Joker kilt him."

"That fuckin' Joker. I didn't see that coming."

Christy shook Batman out of his head, trying to focus. "So we have a go. You distract him. And I hit him."

Little Mike had two legitimate questions. "Distract him with what? And hit him with bloody what?"

Christy looked around. There wasn't much left in the flat

other than the bare essentials. A sofa, fridge, widescreen TV, and PlayStation 2.

He ripped the foam on the sofa arm and yanked out a bit of a plank.

"This for the hitting."

"That?" said Little Mike doubtfully.

"There's a nail in it."

"A nail. Are you de-looo-sional, Christy? Two letters for ye." Little Mike cupped his hands around his mouth. "Pee Jay. We're fucked. We take the breaks and hope there's no freaky stuff."

Christy wouldn't hear it. "No. He comes in this door here, right?"

"*The* door, you mean. The one door."

"So he comes in, and you distract him. Then I fucking whack him straight between the eyes, with the nail. And we're off on the ferry to England. Or down into the deep country. Waterford or something. I heard they got jungles down there, brother. Local natives that will get up on ye for fifty cent. Like fuckin' Mexico."

Little Mike was sucked in by his friend's enthusiasm. "And just how am I supposed to distract him?"

"You know how," said Christy meaningfully, nodding in a respectful and non-homosexual way at Little Mike's bollock area.

"Fuck off," said Mike, cupping said area.

"The big lad has to come out," said Christy. "It's the only extraordinary thing in the flat. It's all we have."

"It's all I have. Fuck off and get yer own."

Little Mike's dick was legendary in the flats, in the entire north side. This was mainly due to the fact that Mike himself had spray-painted every hoarding in Dublin with the legend,

*Little Mike has thirteen inches.* Followed by his mobile number. Morning, noon, and night he was on that phone.

"PJ is bad enough without taunting him. If I have the lad out, it's just rubbing his nose in it. He'll have to cut the big fella off."

Christy had it all figured out. "No. He comes in, expecting two fellas to either have a go, or be shitting themselves in the corner. What he doesn't expect is Mister Thirteen Inches eyeballing him. So for one second, he's off his stride, then I whack him in the face."

Little Mike was a sucker for flattery. "You really think the big fella would put a professional like PJ off?"

Christy snorted. "I fucking know it. Jesus Christ, that thing has a shadow longer than the Spire."

Little Mike was amazed to find himself considering the idea. "Do we have anything? Beer, blow, fucking anything?"

"I think there's a drop of Fanta in the end of that can."

"Ah now, if you're going to start taking the piss, you can show PJ your own langer."

"Sorry, sorry. We've nothing. There's no time anyway. He's nearly here."

It was true. The footsteps were louder now. No echo. PJ would be kicking in the door any second. He was their future and there was no escaping it.

"Over here," ordered Christy, pulling his friend's shoulders. "Right in front of the door."

"And what? Just pull it out through the zip? Or drop the pants altogether."

"I'd say through the zip, in case you have to run." That was Christy, always thinking.

The footsteps were not going up anymore, they were going along.

"Nearly there," said Little Mike. "There's nothing in the bottom of your pocket. A doobie? A pill?"

"Nothing. Believe me."

"Shit. Sorry. Just asking."

Little Mike unzipped, rummaged, and flopped.

Christy had seen it before, but still spared a moment to look.

"Thirteen?"

"Yes, thirteen. Fuck off, begrudger."

"You know, those school rulers have two sides. Centimeters and inches."

Little Mike brandished his weapon. "You couldn't even see the ruler, mate."

PJ was coming. Each footfall firm and confident. He wanted to be heard. Fed on the fear. His legend grew larger with every step.

"Shit, I dunno, brother," said Christy, and it was *his* plan.

Little Mike's phone rang. He managed to answer without fumbling.

"Yes. This is he . . . It's true what it says, amn't I looking at it . . ."

"Mike!" hissed Christy, tapping his watch.

"Ah, yeah. Listen, let me get back to you. We'll have text." This was Little Mike's standard hang-up line. He claimed to have thought of it himself.

Mike opened his knees wide, so that his langer would be framed by the gap between his legs. For first impressions a boner would have been good, but not likely.

"Okay, ready?"

Christy raised the piece of wood, making sure the nail was pointing away from him.

"Ready. This fucker's dead."

A split second later, PJ kicked in the door. He was mildly surprised to see Little Mike before him with his large langer swinging in the breeze, so he mashed it with his boot. And there was Christy, skinny, red mop, tracksuit, waving a piece of furniture at him. PJ caught the plank and reversed it into yer man's face. Two down. No sweat. He brushed a section of the sofa with a sticky fabric roller he always carried, and sat to wait for the boys to stop screaming.

Christy was the first to get a grip.

"We've no candles."

PJ toyed with his bleached goatee. "Your mascara's ruined. You want to get the waterproof kind. My lady says Revlon is the best."

"Thanks," said Christy automatically. There was a red circle in his forehead where the head of the nail had hit him. He looked like he'd been shot.

Little Mike was still wailing, trying to massage some life into his penis. "You don't know what you've done," he sobbed. "You don't know who this is."

PJ rolled his eyes, like a culture-vulture faced with atrocious opera. "Well, I'm guessing that's the legendary thirteen inches I've been reading so much about. You sure you weren't using a metric measuring tape?"

"Might have been," said Little Mike. That's what fear does to a person.

PJ linked his fingers, cracking the knuckles. "So, anyway. Christy boy, you stole from Mister Warren."

Christy tried the *tell the truth* strategy. "One can of Fanta. I forgot where I was."

"Yeah, well, whatever. The closed-circuit camera caught you in the act. So I'm here to make you pay."

"What's a can of Fanta? About a yo-yo?"

"Exactly right. Plus a million euros robbing tax. So if you can give me one million and one euro in cash, right now, I am going to walk out of here and not cut his mickey off and stuff it down your throat."

Little Mike started to cry.

"Little Mike?" said PJ, giving Christy a moment to consider the offer. "That's like an ironic name, isn't it?"

"Yeah," sobbed Mike. "Like Little John in *Robin Hood* was a huge bastard."

PJ took a lock knife from his pocket, flicking out the blade with his thumb. "Guess what they'll be calling you from now on?"

"What?"

"Mike," said PJ, grinning.

His grin grew to a hearty laugh. This was PJ's favorite kind of joke, one pertaining to a brutality he was about to inflict.

He raised a meaty hand, slapping it down on the sofa arm. This was unfortunate, as Christy had earlier pulled out the wooden plank under the foam. One nail had come out with the plank, the rest had stayed in because they were faced the other way.

PJ's arm sank through the slit in the foam and onto half a dozen nails.

The blood drained from his face and began coming out his arm. Orange foam turned red and soggy.

"Heaaaarrgh!" said PJ, who had been trying to say *help*, then lost the run of his brain.

Little Mike was a nice young fella, really. "Jesus Christ. We've got to help him!"

"Blooaaargh!" screamed PJ. More mangled words.

Christy pulled him back. "No. Help him and he'll kill us. How's your mickey?"

Mike examined it gingerly. "I need ice. And a splint."

"There are no bones in your dick."

"Maybe not in *your* dick."

Blood fountained like a fountain of blood. Christy and Mike were showered with sticky droplets. Little Mike picked up an empty cigarette box to reveal a blood-free rectangle below.

"Look," he said. "Remember blow-painting in school?"

They talked about art for a while to take their minds off PJ's screaming. The enforcer tried to free his arm from the nails, but he'd waited too long and hadn't the strength. You could see it in his face, that he didn't believe what has happening.

"But I'm PJ," he muttered, when he could get a sentence together. It was all he said before passing out.

Christy poked PJ's shoulder and got no reaction. "This is worse than the Fanta," he pronounced.

Little Mike was checking his mickey again. "There's a Nike swoosh on me lad."

"I think he's dead. We killed PJ."

Little Mike coiled his member and zipped it away. "No, Christy, he killed himself. It was an accident."

PJ looked dead. His entire shaven head was the color of his bleached goatee, and his tongue lolled out like a movie drunk. Amazing how quickly it could happen. Half a dozen nails in the wrong place.

"Warren will blame us anyway. We're über-fucked now."

*Über-fucked* was one of Christy's sayings, which he claimed to have made up himself but had actually heard it in a blue movie.

Little Mike experimented with walking, cowboy style.

"Okay, so let's get the hell out of here, before the next wave."

Christy straightened his tracksuit, which was his equivalent of packing.

"Okay. We might have a few hours before Warren susses anything. Maybe we could get out on the ring road and hitch a lift to Waterford."

Mike grinned through his pain. "Chill with the señoritas."

"Sí, muchacho."

Christy was smiling a bit wide, so Mike said, "I'm grinning through my pain here, so don't get too fucking happy."

"Sorry, brother."

PJ's phone rang. It was a customized tone to the tune of Chas 'n' Dave's "Rabbit."

"Warren!" said Christy and Little Mike simultaneously.

Christy followed the ring to PJ's jacket pocket and pulled out the phone.

"The new Nokia," said Mike admiringly. "Nice one."

"I gotta answer it," said Christy. "If I don't, Warren will shoot some other wanker over here." He danced around with the phone, as though it were on fire. "I'll pretend I'm PJ. I have a deep voice like him."

"My arse."

"You do it."

"I wouldn't know what to say. I'm no good under pressure."

Christy slapped his own forehead to get the ideas flowing. "Okay. Start screaming!"

"What?"

"Look!" shouted Christy. "PJ's alive!"

Little Mike screamed. Christy answered the phone.

"Y'ello."

Warren sounded pissed off. "What the fuck's going on up there, PJ? Haven't you finished with those two muppets yet?"

Mike screamed again, getting the idea. Camouflage.

"Two minutes, Mister Warren!" shouted Christy.

"Yer not, like, doing anything, are ye? You know, 'cause if you are, make sure to video it, son."

"Will do, Mister Warren."

"Jesus, that fucker can scream. Is that the one with the makeup?"

Christy was wounded. "Shut up, you ugly motherfucking wankstain! Not you, obviously, Mister Warren."

"Obviously."

"No, it's the other one. The one with the big cock."

"Yeah, whatever, just hurry it up. I'm a bit jumpy down here with the night safe bag. You know what the urchins around here are like. No fucking respect."

"On my way, Mister Warren."

Warren hung up, so he could hold onto his money with two hands. Christy dropped PJ's phone back into the dead enforcer's pocket.

"Cheers, brother," he said automatically.

Little Mike took deep whooping breaths. "Jesus. Screaming's not easy."

Christy peered out the flat window. "Warren is below in the car, on his own. With the day's money. Imagine the time we could have in Waterford with that."

Little Mike knew the look on his friend's face. "You're not planning something, are you? Because you know how your plans turn out."

"PJ's dead, isn't he?"

"I hope that's not the case for the defense, because he killed himself. Nothing to do with you. Dumb fucking luck."

"Myaark," said PJ, falling forward from the sofa. His arm

came free with a sound like an oyster being sucked out of a shell.

Christy and Little Mike screamed like school girls and ran straight out the door.

"Arm, fuckaaark!" moaned PJ behind them. A bit less dead than previously believed.

In the corridor Christy was blessed with an idea. Rather than go through the usual discussion rigmarole with Little Mike, he decided to act on his own initiative. After all, Batman occasionally decided to go on missions without Robin. Or he used to, until that bastard Joker came along. Now he had no choice in the matter. Christy pulled out his phone, composing a text on the run. He sent it to every runner in the building who had made drops for him over the past months.

*Bllx n BMW sez Man UTD r shite,* read the message.

In seconds doors were whipped open and enraged Manchester United fans spilled onto the balconies. They howled like hyenas, pouring down the stairwells. Twenty fearless, immortal little fuckers headed straight for Warren's car door.

Christy waved his phone. "I got it too. Some fucker in a BMW hates Man United. Out the front. Big fatheaded cunt."

Little Mike copped on for once, but felt he was being left out. "He said that Andioni fucks pigs. And, eh, sucks shit through straws."

One urchin stopped. He was wearing an Andioni jersey. "I heard about the shit thing. It's homeopathic, for the squirts. It's not his own shit."

Little Mike faltered, then came back with: "Yer man in the BMW says it *is* his own shit."

"Cunt!" spat the urchin, disappearing down the stairwell in a red-and-white flash.

Christy and Little Mike held back, allowing the sea of miniature hooligans to flow around them. Several hands dipped into their pockets, but came out empty. It was like a couple of sharks being nibbled by cleaner fish. If the sharks were scared shitless.

It took a couple of minutes to make it down to the surface, and by then Warren's Beamer was being pelted with everything light enough to throw. A couple of boys had kicked over a few wheelie bins and were firing rotten vegetables.

Warren was not taking it well. He opened the window a crack.

"Fuck off home, ye blackguards!" he roared through the gap, his comb-over separating from his skull. "Don't you know who I am?"

The boy in the Andioni jersey hopped up on his bonnet. "Yeah, Mister. You're the cunt who sucks shit through straws. Your *own* shit."

The boy apparently could not produce a shit on command, but he could certainly have a slash. He undid his fly and pissed in lazy arcs across Warren's windscreen. The wipers sloshing most of it back onto his own trainers did not seem to put him off.

Little Mike and Christy were circling around the back, giggling.

"Warren will do his nut. He's not used to this kind of abuse."

"Serves him right. Him and his fucking tests."

Warren, as predicted, did his nut. He struggled from the passenger seat, waving a large pistol.

"Now who sucks shit? You fucking cockroach."

A few warning shots, thought the drugs-and-porn video baron, just to send these monkeys back to their tree. The reports echoed off the apartment block walls, scattering boys like frightened birds. Except unlike frightened birds, they only scattered as far as the nearest cover, then peeked over for a look at the gun.

Warren, with his flapping hair and Louis Copeland suit, mistook this curiosity for newfound respect.

"That's more like it!" he shouted, waving the pistol. "Now you're getting the idea. Nobody fucks with me on my own doorstep."

One boy yawned. Several more hooted. These were old lines. Rendered impotent by dozens of straight-to-video films.

Christy and Little Mike were thrilled with all this lack of respect. They would have been joining in themselves if they hadn't been sneaking up behind the car.

"He's going to see us," hissed Mike. "We need a distraction. Will I get me lad out again?"

Christy pointed across at the flats. "No. I think we're all right for a distraction."

PJ was stumbling out the door like a zombie, swinging his knife before him like a blind man's cane. His bad arm looked like it had been dipped in crimson paint.

"Mistaaaark," he groaned.

Warren was shocked. "Fuckin' hell, PJ. You didn't go and shove your entire arm up someone's arse, did you?"

Christy and Little Mike didn't hear the reply to this unusual question, because they were in the BMW and reversing across the car park. Warren—fair play to him—reacted quickly enough, putting several rounds into the windscreen.

Mike stuck his head out the side window. "Bullet-proof

glass, asshole. Yer always going on about it." He then with-drew his head sharpish as another bullet whistled past his ear.

Before they pulled onto the road, Christy saw Warren hurl his empty gun in their direction. Not wise. The urchins were on him in under a second, stripping him like piranas on flesh. PJ didn't fare much better. He got a swift kick in the bollocks and his wallet lifted.

"Ah, Jaysus," said Christy regretfully. "We forgot PJ's wallet."

Mike had the night safe bag open on his lap. It was filled with wedges of banded notes.

"We're made, Mike," hooted Christy when he saw the cash. "There must be thirty grand in here. Maybe forty. We can live like kings on this in Waterford. Those señoritas love fellas from the big city. We'll be like Bono and the Edge, brother."

They pulled away from the flats, flashing everyone they thought they might know. In minutes, they were on the motorway heading south.

Christy was already lost in the dream. "Come tomorrow and we'll be topless by the pool. Sipping cocktails in the sunny southeast, a girl on either side and one in the middle."

Little Mike's phone rang.

"Hello. Mike here." He winked at Christy. Another thirteen-inch call. "Yep, it's true. I have it right here before me. Could use a little TLC, as it happens . . . Uhuh . . . Really? Well, I'm sure we could work something out."

Mike covered the mouthpiece with a hand.

"Any chance we could make a stopover in Castledermot?"

# BLACK STUFF
## BY KEN BRUEN

A RT: *skill; human skill or workmanship.*
Then you got a whole page of crap on:

*Art*
*Form*
*Nouveau*
*Paper*
*—ful*

Like I've got the interest.

Jesus.

I was in the bookshop, killing time, saw the manager give me the look. That's why I picked up a book, a goddamn dictionary, weighing like a ton, opened it to the bit on *art*. Glanced up, the manager is having a word with the security schmuck.

Yeah, guys, I'm going to steal the heaviest tome in the shop.

Check my watch, Timex piece of shit, but it's getting late. Tell you one thing, after the job, first item, a gold Rolex. The imitations are everywhere but the real deal . . . ah, slide that sucker on your wrist, dude, you are home.

Cost a bundle, right?

The whole point, right?

On my way out, I touch the manager's arm, the wanker

jumps. I go, "Whoa . . . bit nervous there, pal? Could you help me?"

He has bad teeth, yellow with flecks of green, a little like the Irish flag. He stammered: "How, I mean . . . am . . . *what?*"

"*Dictionary for Dummies*, you got that?"

His body language is assessing me and wanting to roar, "*Nigger!*"

Man, I know it, you grow up black in a town like Dublin, you *know.*

He pulls himself together, those assertive training sessions weren't blown, he gets a prissy clipped tone, asks, "And who would that help, might I inquire?"

"*You*, buddy, you'd really benefit. See, next time a non-Caucasian comes in, you can grab your dummy dictionary, look up . . . *discretion* . . . and if that helps, go for it, check out *assumptions*, too, you'll be a whole new man." I patted his cheek, added: "You might also search for *dentistry*, Yellow Pages your best bet there."

I was in the snug in Mulligans, few punters around.

A guy comes in, orders a drink, American accent but off, as if he'd learned it, says to Jeff, "Gordon's on the rocks, splash of tonic."

Then: "Bud back."

Jeff gives him a look and the guy offers a hearty chuckle, explains, "I mean, *as well as*, guess you folk say . . . *with it* . . . or *in addition to?*" Was he going to give the whole nine?

He got the drinks, walked over, sat at my table, asked, "How you doing?"

Like every night in the city, some asshole does the same Joey Tribiani tired rap. I didn't answer. Instead, I peeled a piece of skin on my thumb. He said, "You don't wanna inflame that, buddy."

*Wanna?*

So I asked, "You a doctor?"

He was delighted, countered, feigning surprise, "You're Irish?" Not believing it, like I'm black, so *come on*. I nod and he takes a hefty slug of the gin, grimaces, then: "How'd that happen?"

I still don't know why but I told him the truth. Usually, who gives a fuck?

Sean Connery said, tell them the truth, then it's their problem. My mother was from Ballymun, yeah, Ireland's most notorious housing estate. Fuck, there's a cliché: She'd a one night stand with a sailor.

How feckin sad is that?

And not a white guy.

He asked, "So, was it, like . . . tough, am . . . ?"

I let that hover, let him taste it, then did the Irish gig, a question with a question. "Being black, or being fatherless?"

He went, "Uh huh."

Noncommital or what?

I said, "Dublin wasn't a city, it was still a town, and a small one, till the tiger roared."

He interrupted: "You're talking the Celtic Tiger, am I right?"

I nodded, continued, "So I was fourteen before I knew I was black, different."

He didn't believe it, asked, "But the kids at school, they had to be on your ass. I mean, gimme a break, buddy."

His glass was empty. I said, "They were *on my ass* because I was shit at hurling."

He stared at his glass, like . . . *where's that go?* Echoed,

"Hurling, that's the national game, yeah?"

I said, "Cross between hockey and murder."

He stood, asked, "Get you a refill there?"

I decided to fuck with him a little, he said, "Large Jameson, Guinness back."

The boilermaker threw him, but he rallied, said, "Me too."

Got those squared away, raised the amber, clinked my glass, and you guessed it, said, "Here's looking at you, pal."

Fuck on a bike.

The other side of the whiskey, I climbed down a notch, eased, but not totally.

He was assessing me, covertly, then: "Got some pecs on you there, fella. Hitting the gym, huh?"

He was right. Punishing program, keep the snakes from spitting, the ones in my head, the shrink had said. *"You take your meds, the snakes won't go away—we're scientists, not shamans—but they will be quieter."*

Shrink humor?

I quit the meds. Sure, they hushed the reptiles, but as barter, took my edge. I'd done some steroids, got those abs swollen, but fuck, it's true, they cut your dick in half. And a black guy with shrinkage? . . . Depths of absurdity.

I was supping the Guinness, few better blends than the slow wash over Jameson. I said, "Yeah, I work out."

He produced a soft pack of Camels, gold Zippo, then frowned, asked, "You guys got the no-smoking bug? . . . It's illegal in here?" Like he didn't know already. Then reached out his hand, said, "I'm Bowman, Charlie, my buddies call me Bow."

I'm thinking, *Call you arsehole.*

And he waits till I extend my hand, the two fingers visibly crushed. He clocks them, I say, "Phil."

He shakes my hand, careful of the ruined fingers, goes for levity, asks, "Phil, that it, no surname? C'mon buddy, we're like bonding, am I right? How can I put it, *Phil* me in?" He laughed, expecting me to join.

I didn't.

I said, "For Phil Lynott, Thin Lizzy. You heard Lynott speak, his Dublin accent was near incomprehensible, but when he sang, pure rock. Geldof said Phil was the total rock star, went to bed in the leather trousers."

Bow's mouth was turned down. He said, "My taste runs more to Van Morrison."

Figured.

He spotted the book on the seat beside me, Bukowski, asked, "That's yours, you're into . . . Buk?"

*Buk?*

Fucksakes.

My mother, broke, impoverished, sullen, ill, had instilled: *"Never, and I mean never, let them know how smart you are."*

Took me a long time to assimilate that, too long. The days after her funeral, I'd a few quid from the horses, got a mason to carve:

I

DIDN'T

LET

THEM

KNOW

Like that.

The mason, puzzled, asked, "The hell does that mean?" I gave him the ice eyes, he muttered, "Jeez, what's wrong with *Rest in peace?*" I said, "That's what it means, just another

form." He scratched his arse, said, "Means shite, you ask me."
He said this *after* I paid him.

So I threw a glance at the Bukowki. Denied him, going,
"Not mine. I need books with, like, pictures."

Bow and I began to meet, few times a week, no biggie, but it
grew. Me, careful to play the dumbass, let him cream on his
superiority. He paid the freight, I could mostly listen.

A month in, he asked, "You hurting there, Phil?"

I was mid-swallow, my second pint. I stopped, put the
glass down, asked, "What?"

His eyes were granite, said, "Bit short on the readies . . .
Hey, I'm not bitching."

. . . (*Oh yeah?*)

"But there's no free lunch. You familiar with that turn
of phrase, black guy? When we freed your asses, we figured
you might be self-sufficient. Maybe spring for the odd
drink?"

I was thinking of how my mother would love this prick.
He tapped his empty glass twice, then, "You're good company,
Phil, not the brightest tool in the box. This ride's, like, com-
ing to a halt."

I was trying to rein it in, not let the snakes push the glass
into his supercilious mouth, especially when he added: "You
getting this? *Earth to Leroy*, like . . . hello?"

I was massaging my ruined fingers, remembering . . . One
of the first jobs I did, driver for a post office stunt. I was
younger, and dare I say . . . *greener?*

The outfit were northeners, had lost their driver at the
last minute. How I got drafted.

They came out of the post office in Malahide, more a
suburb of Dublin now, guns above their heads, screaming like

banshees, piled into the back. The motor stalled. Only two minutes, but it was a long 120 seconds. By the Grand Canal, the effluent from the Liffey smelling to high heaven. Changing cars, they held me down, crushed my fingers, using the butt of a shotgun, the Belfast guy going, "*Two minutes you lost, two fingers you blow.*"

I stared at Bow, asked, "You have something in mind?"

The Zippo was flat on the table, I could see a logo: *Focus.*

He indicated it, said, "That's the key. I'm thinking you could do with a wedge, a healthy slab of tax-free euros."

Jeez, he was some pain in the arse, but I stayed . . . *focused?* . . . below radar, asked, "Who doesn't?"

Looked like he might applaud, then, "I'm taking a shot here, but I'm figuring you know zilch about art."

I stayed in role, asked, "Art who?"

Didn't like it, I noticed. When he was bothered as he was now, the accent dipped. I smiled, thinking, *Not so focused now, and certainly not American.*

He gritted his teeth, grunted, "Art is . . . everything. All the rest is . . . a support system."

I leaned on the needle, said, "You like art, yeah?"

Thought he might come across the table, but he reined in, took a breath, a drink, said in a patient clipped tone, "Lesson one, you don't *like* art, you *appreciate* it."

I kept my eyes dull, and that's an art.

He snapped, "You want to pay attention, fella, maybe you can learn something. I'm going to tell you about one of the very finest, Whistler."

I resisted the impulse to put my lips together and like . . . blow.

He began: "There is a portrait by him, a 'painted tribute to a gentle old lady.' The lady looks old, but that's because he was old when he did it. A time, 1871, when the railroads were about to replace the covered wagons. You see a white light wall, then . . .

"Straight curtain . . .

"Straight baseboard . . .

"Chair, footrest . . . *straight* . . .

"Everything is straightened out, the only roundness is her face. He titled it, *Arrangement in Gray and Black*. Moving along, you'll see a silk curtain, in Japanese style, with a butterfly as decoration—his tribute to a country he admired. There's a picture on the wall, and this is significant, as it's the brightest white spot in the painting. The woman's hands are white, her handkerchief is white, contrasting the black dress. Her bonnet has different shades to make her face benign, kindly. The entire ensemble is an homage to this lady, his mother, whom he adored."

He waffled on for maybe another ten minutes, then finally stopped. Looked at me. I was going to go, *I'm straight*, but instead asked, "I need to know this . . . why?"

Now he smiled, said, "Because you and me, buddy, we're going to steal it."

The Musée d'Orsay had loaned it to the city of Dublin for six months. Had been on display for three now . . . in Merrion Square, the posh area of the city—a detail of Army and Gardaí were keeping tabs. Once the initial flush of interest and fanfare died down, the crowds dropped off. More important events like the hurling final, race meetings, took precedence. Security, though in evidence, was more for show than intent. An indication of the public losing interest, the picture had been moved to Parnell Square, the other side of the Liffey, damnation in itself.

Bow said, "Lazy fuckers, last week they didn't even bother to load the CCTV."

"How do you know?" I asked. And got the frost smile, superior and not a mile from aggressive.

He used his index finger to tap his nose, said, "A guy on the museum staff? He's got himself a little problem."

Did he mean cocaine or curiosity?

He continued: "I've helped him . . . get connected . . . and he's grateful . . . and now he's vulnerable. In ten days there will be a window in the security—the patrol is to be switched, the CCTV is to be revamped, there'll only be two guys on actual watch. Can you fucking believe it?"

We hadn't had a drink for over half an hour, the lecture was lengthy, so I injected a touch of steel, asked, "And the two, the ones keeping guard, they're going to what, give it to us?"

Now he laughed, as if he'd been waiting for an excuse. "How fucking stupid are you?" Shaking his head, like good help was hard to find, he said, "We're going to give them the gas."

That's what we did.

Dream job—in, out. No frills, no flak.

. . . Unless you count the dead guy.

We'd donned cleaner's gear, always wanted to *don* something, gives that hint of gravitas. Bow said, "Help us blend."

Especially in my case, sign of the new Ireland, black guy riding a mop, no one blinked an eye.

We'd become America.

Them janitor blues, pushing dee broom, miming dee black and sullen—translate: invisible.

The guards, one in mid-yawn. We hit them fast, tied

them up, tops, four minutes. I didn't glance at the painting, was fearful it might remind me of my mother. Bow did, I heard the catch in his breathing. Then we were almost done, reached the back door, when a soldier came out of nowhere, a pistol in his hand, roared, "Hold on just a bloody minute!"

Bow shot him in the gut. I'd been going for the gas. I stared at Bow, whined, "No need for that."

The smirk, his mouth curled down, he put two more rounds in the guy, asked, "Who's talking about *need*?"

The heat came down
    Hard
    Relentless
    Like the Dublin drizzle, rain that drove Joyce to Switzerland
    With
    . . . Malice aforethought.

We kept a low-to-lowest profile. A whole month before we met for the split, the rendezvous in an apartment on Pembroke Road, not far from the American embassy, an area I'd have little business in. Bow had rented the bottom floor, wide spacious affair, marred by filth, empty takeaway cartons, dirty plates in the sink, clothes strewn on the floor, the coffee table a riot of booze. He was dressed, I kid you not, in a smoking jacket, like some Agatha Christie major. Not even David Niven could pull that gig off.

Worse: on the pocket, the letter . . . *B*.

For . . . *Bollocks?*

He was wearing unironed tan cords and flip-flops, the sound slapping against the bare floor. I was wearing a T, jeans, Nike trainers with the cushion sole. A logo on my T . . . *Point Blankers*.

Near the window was the painting, dropped like an afterthought. I took my first real appraisal. The old lady did indeed look . . . old. She was nothing like my mother—my mother had never sat down in her wretched life.

I heard the unmistakable rack of a weapon and turned to see Bow holding a pistol. He said, "Excuse the mess, but decent help, man, it's impossible to find."

I stared at the gun, asked, "You're not American, right?"

Winded him, came at him from left field, I added: "You're good most of the time, you've it down and tight, almost pull it off but it slips, couple of words blow the act."

His eyes gone feral, he moved the weapon, pointing at the center of my chest, asked, "What fucking words?"

I sighed theatrically (is there any other way?), said, "Okay, you say . . . *mighty, fierce* . . ."

He put up his left hand. Not going to concede easy, protested, "Could have picked them up, been here a time."

I nodded, then, "But you use *fierce* in both senses, like *terrific*, and like *woesome*—gotta be Irish to instinctively get that. You can learn the sense of it, but never the full usage."

He went to interrupt but I shouted, "Hey, I'm not done! The real giveaway, apart from calling a pint a *pint of stout*, is *me fags* . . . Americans are never going to be able to call cigarettes *gay*."

He shrugged, let it go, said, "Had you going for a while, yeah?"

I could give him that, allowed, "Sure, you're as good as the real thing."

Used the gun to scratch his belly, said, "Long as we're confronting, you're not Homer Simpson either, not the dumb schmuck you peddle. The Bukowski, it was yours, and the way you didn't look at the painting, you'd have to be real smart not to show curiosity."

I reached in my pocket, registered his alarm, soothed, "It's a book, see . . ." Took out the Bukowski, *Ham on Rye*, flipped it on the floor, said, "A going-away present, because we're done, right?"

As if I hadn't noticed the weapon. His grip on the butt had eased, not a lot but a little. He said, "In the bedroom I got near thirty large, you believe that, nigger?"

No matter how many times I hear the word, and I hear it plenty, it is always a lash coming out of a white mouth, an obscenity. He let it saturate, then added, "I got enough nose candy to light up O'Connell Street for months, soon as I deliver the painting and get the rest of the cash. A serious amount, but guess what, I'm a greedy bastard, I don't really share." Pause, then, "And share with a darkie? . . . Get real. Gotta tell you, I'm a supporter of the Klan—did you know they were founded by a John Kennedy? How's that for blarney?"

I lowered my head, said, "Never let the left hand see what—"

Shot him in the face, the gun in my right hand, almost hidden by the crushed fingers. The second tore through his chest. I said, Brooklyn inflection, "Duh, you gotta . . . *focus.*"

Got the cash, put the portrait under my coat, didn't look back. Near Stephen's Green a wino was sprawled beside a litter bin. I gave him some notes and stuffed the Whistler in the bin. He croaked, "No good, huh?"

I said, "It's a question of appreciation."

# TRIBUNAL
BY PAT MULLAN

T*here's a buzz about the place. Sure as hell wasn't here when I left fifteen years ago.* He remembered Dublin as the pits then. Dark, priest-ridden, can't-do culture, living on government handouts and money from the emigrants. A Godforsaken hole of a place. For himself, anyway. Edmund Burke. *Yeah, that's me. My old man had delusions. Thought if he named me after the great Irish statesman that the name would overcome the bad genes and the lousy upbringing.* Willie Burke had been a failure, failed at every no-risk job he ever attempted, and the old man had ended his days earning a mere pittance as a salesman in a tailoring shop that had seen its best days in the last century. Mass on Sunday was the highlight of his mother's week, a timid woman from the west of Ireland who'd never felt at home in the big city. An only child, Edmund had been conceived just as his mother's biological clock was about to stop ticking. She was forty-two when she had him.

All these things flooded his mind as he jumped into the taxi at Dublin Airport and told the driver to take him to Ballsbridge. He'd survived. Succeeded because his father's failure terrified him. Got into Trinity, earned a law degree, headed for England, stayed a year in a boring clerk job at a London legal firm as resident Paddy. Luck intervened. His mother's uncle in Boston sponsored him to the States. Decided that he'd go by sea instead of air. Took a 28,000-ton liner out of Liverpool. Gave him a sense of being a pilgrim setting out for the New World.

Now he was back. Why. The Celtic Tiger! That's why. Well, one of the reasons. He was running away again. But that's another story. Taking a year off from his New York law firm. Had just about enough of his mob clients. As well as his ex who wanted to rob him blind. Oh yeah, he'd stashed away a few dollars, but still hadn't made that million. Maybe Dublin's the place to be these days. Everybody's here. All these faces in Dublin on a Tuesday and you see them again in New York or L.A. on the weekend. Aidan Quinn. Gabriel Byrne. Liam Neeson. Colin Farrell. Michael Flatley now a household name with *Riverdance* conquering the world. And Michael O'Leary and Ryanair conquering the skies. The priests are scarce on the ground these days. Divorce is legal. The Bishop of Galway has a love child with an American lover, and the President of Ireland has crossed the religious divide to take communion in a Protestant cathedral. The IRA is about to call it quits and the border separating the Republic from Northern Ireland is gradually becoming an imaginary line. Money talks. And money goes where it's well treated. And the Celtic Tiger is treating it well.

*Money! That's really why I'm here*, he reminded himself. *Not here to feel sentimental. Still, the old city looks good*, he thought. *New roads, new houses, construction cranes everywhere. Plenty of Mercs and BMWs. They're not taking the Liverpool boat anymore. No! They're in investment banking, working for McKinsey and Microsoft. Turning Ireland into the largest exporter of computer software outside of the United States.*

At Ballsbridge, Burke paid the taxi fare and walked up Shelbourne Road. Dublin 4. The most sought after neighborhood in the city. Bright skies and the early morning briskness countered his lack of sleep. Old stately homes lined the streets. Surrounded by sturdy stone walls, they exuded wealth and power. As a kid this would have been an alien place to him. *Still is*, he thought, as he reached a modern four-story apartment block in Ballsbridge Gardens. He already had a key, mailed to him in New York before he'd left.

Once inside, he realized that he could be anywhere. Luxury that would be right at home on Fifth Avenue. He dropped his bags, started the coffee machine, and minutes later sat in the large Jacuzzi bathtub watching the bubbles welcome him to Dublin.

Refreshed and dressed, he arrived at Lillie's Bordello at 6:00. The most elite club in Dublin. Had he been here a few nights ago, after the Irish Film and Television Awards, he could have joined Pierce Brosnan and James Nesbitt as they sang "Danny Boy" at the piano in the VIP room.

This was Murphy's idea. Drop him into the deep end. Meet who's who in Dublin society. Hit the ground running! That's always been Murphy's modus operandi. Murphy was his old law school buddy at Trinity and the reason he'd returned to Dublin. Murphy had built a successful legal business, rich from tribunal money and litigation. Now, with more business than he could handle, he'd developed a distrust for his partners.

It didn't take much persuasion to tempt Ed Burke back to Dublin. His mob clients were a little annoyed at the moment. One with a bullet behind his ear in a ditch in Westchester. Another behind bars on a federal indictment for corruption.

*Jesus Christ! I really could be in New York or L.A.! The same confidence. The same body movements. Damn it. Even the accents are mid-Atlantic.*

All the right people at tonight's reception for a noble cause. Charity. Aid for Africa. Medicine for Chernoble. Sexy stuff. Good publicity for the rich and powerful.

He felt a finger trace its way up his spine, lingered to enjoy, then turned slowly and came face-to-face with her.

"Edmund," she said, moving to within inches. No one else except his mother called him Edmund.

Just then Murphy arrived with drinks. "Ah, a reunion, you two . . . okay! Okay!" he protested their stares, then handed Burke his drink and moved on. But the spell had been broken.

"Pia, it's been a long time," said Ed, looking at the woman who had broken his heart. Days and nights of endless love-making when they both attended Trinity. Summers in Donegal. Running naked into the sea on the Fanad beach at midnight. Dark, Latin beauty, born in Barcelona, Irish father, Spanish mother. Something Irish flashing through, the same way you see the Irish in Anthony Quinn's Mexican face.

"Twenty years, Edmund. You're looking well. If I'd known you were going to be such a success . . ." She let the sentence hang in the air.

Ed wanted to hold her, kiss her, take her to that Fanad beach again. His mind spoke to him: *Oh, Pia, I loved you so much. And you left me for that geek. Now he's one of the top Ministers in the government. Being touted as a future Taoiseach. Speak of the devil.* The man himself approached.

"Ed, I see you're back. Good. We need your talent here. Building a great country these days."

"Well, I'm looking forward to it, Minister. Had things looked like this twenty years ago, I might never have left."

"Well, you're back. That's what matters."

Looking at his wife, he said, "Pia, you and Ed are old friends. Introduce him around. New blood he should meet here." And with that he was gone. Working the audience. Consolidating his mandate.

Ed Burke knew that it was a mistake. But he was addicted. Always had been. In the days that followed, he and Pia threw caution to the wind. They were inseparable and indiscrete. Glued together in cozy corners in the best pubs and clubs, unabashedly naked in private saunas. It seemed their passion had only been fueled by the passing of time.

Just three weeks after his arrival, Ed Burke found himself "in at the deep end," defending Dan Mortimer, one of Dublin's elite, against a class action suit brought by a rabble of welfare-dependent inner-city denizens. As Murphy had said, "Good way to announce your presence to the world. This is a case you can't lose. And making an ally out of Mortimer will seal your career. Besides, it'll be great PR for our firm."

Some said that Mortimer was the public face of the Celtic Tiger. A good quarter of the construction cranes crisscrossing the Dublin skyline bore the Mortimer name in huge capital letters. The new dockland development had Mortimer stamped all over it. But this case had aroused the emotions of the people. The class action suit claimed that Mortimer had illegally acquired derelict inner-city land that should have been used for the community, and had then used his influence to have it rezoned for commercial purposes. Site development had commenced, excessive noise polluted the air, cracks had appeared in the foundation of adjacent houses. The suit also claimed that Mortimer had used aggressive tactics to persuade local homeowners to sell and leave so that he could demolish their homes and make way for further commercial usage. Two hungry young lawyers represented the claimants.

*Just like me twenty years ago,* thought Burke, *idealistic and naïve.* They could not support their case with solid evidence. They promised to produce a witness who would testify that Mortimer had made illegal payments to someone in government to get the land rezoned. But the witness did not show up in court. The judge gave them a second chance. Produce the witness within one week, otherwise the court finds the claim unsubstantiated.

A late-evening wind blew the rain into Burke's face as he stood on the corner awaiting the taxi he'd ordered. It had been a long day in court and he felt uneasy about the whole business. New York was different. There, he knew the good guys from the bad guys. Everything was direct. In your face. Here, nothing resembled that. Too much gray, too little black and white. This country thrived on ambivalence.

An elderly man approached him. Something familiar searched his brain for a memory, a connection.

"Hello, Eddie."

The *Eddie* completed the circuit in his brain. He hadn't been called Eddie since he was a little boy. Marty, Marty Rainey. Age now hid the vitality he remembered. Marty had been almost a surrogate father. Often there for him when his own father was down in the pub in the evening.

"Marty! Is it you?"

"'Tis indeed. Not as supple as you remember. But the old head still works."

"Marty, it's just great seeing you again."

"Eddie, I need to talk to you. It's life or death for me."

Saying it so matter-of-factly took the surprise out of it. The taxi pulled up, saving Ed from looking lost. He insisted on taking Marty home.

As the taxi pulled out into rush hour traffic, Marty said: "I'm your witness."

For a moment Ed Burke was mystified. Then it struck him that Marty's telling him that he's the missing witness at the trial. Ed gripped Marty's arm and looked at him. Marty continued: "I couldn't show up. They threatened me. Told me that I'd wind up in the Liffey. They meant it, Eddie. I suppose I'm a coward."

"Who threatened you, Marty?"

"Thugs! That's who. You don't think they do their own dirty work, do you? No, they hired a bunch of thugs who don't give a shite. They'd kill me as easily as look at me."

"Who ordered it, Marty?"

"Come on, you know who. You're defending one of them in court. I suppose you're gettin' well paid for that. But you've forgotten where you came from, Eddie."

"Damn it, Marty! Don't fucking lecture me. If you're telling me the truth, then you were the bagman for these bastards for years. Selling your own people down the drain."

"You're right. I was stupid. Gambling, bookies, the horses. I owed too much and they paid it off. But believe me, Eddie, I never thought they'd turn our own people out of their homes. I didn't know. Now I want to get them. The bastards. They destroyed me and I want to destroy them."

He reached inside his coat and pulled out a large bulky envelope.

"Everything's in here. All the evidence. Record of pay-offs—who, where, and when. Bank account statements showing how the money was laundered. There's enough here to start a dozen tribunals. It'll destroy Mortimer and bring down the Minister. He's a corrupt bastard! The word around is that you're pretty close with his missus. Watch yourself."

Ed Burke sat in silence, holding the envelope as though it was a bomb. Which, in a sense, it was.

Before he could gather his thoughts, the taxi stopped outside Marty's front door in Harold's Cross. Marty gripped his hand, said, "Do the right thing, Eddie," and left.

And Ed Burke did the right thing. He met next day with Murphy and told him that he could not defend Mortimer, told him about Marty Rainey's evidence, told him that they'd have to meet with the judge and turn this evidence over to the court. Murphy reluctantly agreed and insisted that Burke secure the envelope with the firm for safekeeping until they could take it to court. Burke considered this advice sensible and lodged the envelope in the firm's safe. Had he examined the evidence more thoroughly before he handed it over, he would have seen that Murphy's "fingerprints" were all over the money-laundering operation, tying him directly to the illegal lodgement of these monies offshore in the Ansbacher Cayman accounts.

That same night, the jarring ringing of his phone brought Ed Burke out of a deep slumber. He growled: "Yeah?"

"Ed Burke? Is this Ed Burke?"

"What do you want? Do you know what time it is?"

"This is the emergency call service. We have an alert on Martin Rainey. We think he has fallen in his home and can't get up. He needs help. Can you go there now?"

"But I'm not on any alert system."

"You're on it, Mr. Burke. Mr. Rainey insisted that we call you if he needed help."

Ed Burke decided that he had no choice. Marty Rainey wouldn't have put him on the alert list without a good reason. He confirmed Marty's address with the emergency service, dressed, and called a taxi.

At 3 a.m. with no traffic on the streets, the taxi reached Harold's Cross in fifteen minutes and dropped Burke at the end of Marty's street. A neat row of red brick houses wound in an arc ahead of him; houses that cost a few thousand only fifteen years ago now ran into hundreds of thousands. A cat scurried across the street in front of him, breaking the silence of the night.

He found number 27 and rang the doorbell. No answer. He rang it again, holding down the buzzer. Still no answer. Now he stood contemplating what he should do. He knew that he must get inside. Further down the street he saw a break in the pattern of the houses and what seemed to be a large commercial doorway. Counting the houses he reached it and got lucky. A smaller door stood closed but unlocked. He took out his flashlight, opened the door, and passed through a dry stone wall, finding himself in an open grassy space at the rear of the houses. Counting back he reached Marty's house. The dry stone wall at the back provided a natural foothold. He climbed up. Marty's house, probably his kitchen, had been extended and took up the small backyard. Its flat roof backed up against the wall. Burke simply stepped onto it, reached up, and leveraged himself on a ledge outside the window on the second floor. His luck held. The window stood slightly ajar. He squeezed inside, shined his flashlight around, and saw that he stood on a landing at the head of the stairs.

Calling out Marty's name, he inched his way down the stairs to the living room, found the light switch, and turned it on. He saw the blood first. Pooled around Marty's head where he lay on his side in the middle of the room. A huge open gash crossed his forehead. Burke knelt down and took his pulse. No sign of life. He turned him over to try CPR, and that's when he found that this had been no accident. Marty's throat had been cut.

Burke waited till the ambulance and the Gardaí arrived and sealed off the house. As it was a crime scene, Marty would stay right where he lay until the state pathologist arrived. The Gardaí took a statement from Burke and he left.

Burke made it back to his apartment by 4:30 a.m. Too wired to sleep, he headed for the whiskey. Half a bottle later, he sank into a deep stupor.

*Pia! Pia!* Ed Burke agonized about what to do. In days the scandal would break. The Minister's career would crash. In public. And Pia would crash too. Every tabloid would exploit the story. Exploit her!

Thoughts bounced wildly around his head: *I've got to do something. Got to protect her. But how? I could leave again. Go back to the States. Take her with me. Start a new life with her. Agh, wishful thinking! It's too late for us. Pia won't leave Dublin. It's the center of her world. All the world comes to Dublin now. So what's the incentive to leave? Why should I leave again? Got to brave this thing out.*

Still, Pia had to be warned. He had to tell her what was coming. Get her to leave the Minister. Get out first. Make the first move. Yes, that's what she had to do. And he'd help her. Once he had decided, Burke took action. Dialed her mobile. She picked up immediately.

"Edmund, it's only 9 a.m."

"Pia, let's run away together. Now."

"Oh, Edmund. How I wish."

"Look, it's Friday. I'm off today. Let's go somewhere. Get away from it all. Can you break all your social commitments?"

"Yes! Yes! Yes!"

"Okay, great. I'll make the arrangements. Pick you up by noon."

Murphy met the Minister in Buswells Bar, where all the members of the Dail went for their regular tipple. The Minister asked, "What'll it be, the usual?" and ordered two Jamesons with water chasers.

No preamble for the Minister, he went right for the jugular: "If he brings me down, you go too."

Murphy said nothing.

"Did you hear me? You go too."

"Goddamnit, he's my friend. Isn't there any other way? We could persuade him to lay off."

"Persuade, my ass. Do you realize he's been fucking Pia since he got back?"

"I hate to say it, but . . ."

"Yeah, do you think I'm dumb? I know she's been screwing the world for the past five years. Well, it's over. She won't be making a fool of me anymore."

"What do you mean?"

"Killing two birds with one stone. That's what I mean."

"Jesus, you're crazy. I want no part of it."

"In for a penny, in for a pound. You knew that. Do you really want to lose the mansion in Howth, the little hideaway in Shady Lane where you entertain your Caribbean beauties, your yacht and your membership in the Royal Cork . . . ? Fuck no, you don't want to lose any of it. And you don't want a tribunal looking into everything while you rot your arse in Mountjoy."

Murphy shut up and gulped down his Jameson. Just as quickly another, a double, appeared in front of him. He had to admit to himself that there was no way out. Ed Burke was an investment that he couldn't afford.

Burke chose well. *Get the hell out of Dublin*—the first command he issued to himself. *Go west, young man,* said Horace Greeley in America. And that's what Burke did. Go west to Galway. He knew exactly where. *St. Cleran's.* Once the Galway home of film director John Huston, the place where Angelica spent her childhood. Been turned into a most exclusive guesthouse by another famous Irish-American, Merv Griffin. Just the place for them, away from their Dublin 4 crowd. Time to tell Pia, time to hold her, time to decide.

At St. Cleran's Ed told Pia about the scandal that would break in the days ahead. He teased out all their options, all their choices. And Pia agreed to leave the Minister as soon as they returned to Dublin. Brave out the turbulence ahead. They retired early, Pia reminding him that they had run away together.

Much later they noticed the bottle of Chablis, sitting invitingly in a crystal cooler. Into their second glass, Ed began to feel drowsy and saw that Pia had already closed her eyes and sunk into the pillow beside him. Moments later, he followed her.

Burke's eyes hurt. Bad. His head hurt too. Worse. He tried to open his eyes. Couldn't. Sunlight grilled him through the open blinds. Eyes closed, fighting to stay awake, he slid out of bed, stood up, and felt his way to the window. Gripping the blinds, he yanked them closed and then risked opening his eyes. They still hurt but he could see. Turning around, he stopped dead, halfway between the window and the bed. Pia lay there, naked, one leg dangling on the floor, a trickle of blood from her lips forming a small red pond between her breasts.

# PART II

THE MANHATTAN CONNECTION

# PORTRAIT OF THE KILLER
# AS A YOUNG MAN

BY REED FARREL COLEMAN

J aysus Christ, I hate feckin' Americans! The donkeys
worst among 'em. And them arse-licking cops worst of
all. Them with their fifty-two paychecks and pensions,
their red noses and "Danny Boy" tears. They think glen
to glen is a conversation of like-named punters. Cunts, every
last one. Them that sees romance in the famine and the troubles. Yah, romance in a bloody holocaust and the smell of
cordite in the streets of Derry. And they ease their guilt and
fancy themselves Provo men because they open their wallets
and sing Pogues songs and drown themselves in pubs with a
gold harp above the threshold. What a load a shite.

Oh, and how they imagine us Irish in the worst possible
sense; a race of toothless spud farmers in white cableknit
sweaters and black rubber boots, spouting Joyce or Yeats,
herding lambs with a switch in one hand and a pint of
Guinness in the other. And what of our race of red-haired
colleens? Why, they're out in lush pastures in their white
blouses and green plaid skirts gathering clover and hunting
for pots of gold. Bollix!

I hadn't meant to kill the first one. I had dreamed of it,
for sure. Taking one of the cheery bastards who hopped into
me cab and opening him up like an Easter lamb, tossing his
innards out my windows as I drove the M-road back from
Shannon. But like with sex, it never quite happens the way

you dream it. I s'pose if I had planned it, it would never have come off at all. I had sat patiently for a year at the wheel and listened to my American cousins affect cartoon brogues, recite bad jokes, and spew inanities at the back of me head.

"Would you like a seven-course Irish meal? A six-pack and a patata."

"Top a the mernin' to ya, boyo."

"Where do you keep the leprechauns? In the trunk?"

"Hey, where's me Lucky Charms?"

"Is it true about the Irish Curse?"

"You don't have red hair!"

"Irish Spring. Sure it smells good on him, but I like it too."

What eejits!

I took all of it and more; let it build up like steam in the kettle. It got so that the loathing felt warm as the shame of me Irish blood. I learned to bathe in it so that the thought of killing one of me American fares made me hard as a hurly soaked through with water and left to cure in a baking hot oven. Hate had always been a comfort to me. What's more natural than hate, save rage? I hate Pakis, tinkers even more. But nothing I had known before compared to how I hated Americans. It was my coming of age.

Then, out of the blue, I was triggered. A blowsy Yank, all muzzy and hog-eyed, got in me cab just outside Davy Byrne's Pub in Duke Street and asked to go to the Gresham Hotel in O'Connell Street Upper. He went quiet on me after first announcing he was ex of the NYPD. As if I gave a shite. For fuck's sake, did he expect me to kiss his ring? So many sheets to the wind was he that he seemed to lose his voice as well as his senses. Then catching his breath, he began to rant about the weather, but that isn't what set me off.

No—it was when he complained bitterly that us Irish drive as the Brits do, on the wrong side of the road. In America, he assured me, they would never put up with that shit. It was at that point I decided to no longer put up with his. Well, it wasn't so much a decision as a reflex. Why, of all things that should have lit my candle, I cannot say, but light it it did.

I detoured to a section of town where, at that hour, there would likely be no foot traffic at all. Feigning illness, I pulled into an alley near dark as my heart. I got out of the cab, having already slid me sawed-off baseball bat up me trouser leg. When he came to look after me as I knelt on the cobbles pretending to retch up me lungs, I slammed the bat into his shins with such fury to snap at least one. I nearly orgasmed at the crackle of his shattering bone. He tumbled mightily, his head smacking a brick wall. *Thud* does not describe the sound of his skull against the stone. He was not dead, only damaged. I made sure to damage him well beyond dead. His face, what there was left of it, now red from blood and not from drink. I removed his watch, his jewelry, credit cards, the money from his wallet. I learned that from American TV.

"Was that a home run, fella?" I asked, tossing his pilfered wallet onto his body.

He was strangely silent.

There have been five more like him spread out over the last two years. I've made certain to alter the way in which I approach my victims, never again picking one up in me cab. They're such suckers for the glad hand and blarney that there's no challenge in it. They're kittens to cream. Nor have I repeated the method I've used to murder them. I've stabbed one, poisoned another, beaten one to death with me fists, strangled one, and used a shotgun on the last. When the Gardaí seemed to be putting two and two together, not usually a skill they possess, I was forced to kill at random. Not a drop of red, white, or blue involved.

She was an Irish girl, pretty enough to interest the press. She was at Trinity studying some wanker named Kant. Had to swallow the laughter on hearing that. Dropped two rufies in her drink, diddled her every way to Sunday, and stabbed her with the same knife I used to do in the American. I cut her in just the same way as I did the Yank. I think of him as the Ugly American. Looked better when I was done with him than when I began.

I feel bad about her sometimes, like when I'm getting meself off. She's the only one I rue. Might have been a future for me with her and Kant, but I had to confuse the Gardaí. Worked like a charm. They need a new calculator. I figure I'll have to do the odd one every now and again. No more pretty girls, though. No philosophy students. Kants, the bunch of them. I'll have to use that line. You think?

*Shite, a fare out in front of Kavanagh's Pub and I was having a tickle with you lot. Do me the favor of keeping your gobs shut until I rid meself of the fare. Then we can get back to our business.*

"Where to, sir?"

"Just drive. I'll tell ya when to stop."

"American?"

"Yeah."

*Jaysus, I finally got a quiet one. No jokes nor brogues. And look at the face on him, Irish as a Galway swan and dour as a priest out of sacramental wine. I almost feel sorry for this one.*

"Here on business or pleasure, you don't mind my asking?"

"Business."

"What kinda business you in?"

"Cop. I'm a cop."

*Fuck on a bike! An American cop, but nothing like the others. He didn't even tell me where. Usually takes no more than a few seconds in me backseat before they show me their friggin' shield and tell me how long till they're vested in their bloody pensions. Then it's to the war stories. As if I give a toss.*

"Collins," I said, reaching me right mitt across my body and over the seat.

"Jack," he said, giving me hand a quick, uncomfortable shake.

*Again, nothing like the others. All the others near crushed me hand, refusing to give it back until I pled for its release. Now as I see him in me rearview, I'd say he's had a fair amount of drink, but he's far from scuppered. He's in turmoil, for sure, by the look on his face. Christ and His blessed mother, damned if I'm not concerned for the bastard.*

"Is everything right by you, Jack?"

"Far from it, Collins."

"Is there anything I can do to ease your troubles, sir?"

"Yeah, can you pull over here? I'm feeling sick."

"It's a rough part of the old town, Jack. Are you sure you can't hold—"

"Pull over!"

*Shite! Now he's out of me cab and down a blind foukin' alley. It's been five minutes. Ah, let me go see how the poor bastard's doing.*

*Thwack!*

"Sorry, Collins."

*Thwack.*

"It's nothing personal, but some shanty prick beat my father to death with a baseball bat down an alley not too far from here."

*Thwack.*

"I figured we owed you cocksuckers one."

*Thwack.*

"Shit, Collins, if I didn't know better, I'd swear you were smiling at me. Fuck you, asshole!"

*Thwack.*

Like I say, I hate Americans, arse-licking cops worst of all.

# THE BEST PART
BY PETER SPIEGELMAN

For Jimmy Lowe, this was the best part—the two of them just out of the shower, wrapped in hotel terrycloth, smelling of expensive shampoo, heat clinging to their bodies like another skin, and his head in her lap. He wasn't sober—he'd more or less given up on that—but for the moment the world wasn't sliding away beneath him. He wasn't rested either, but neither was he wired, or nodding out, or stupid drooling. What he was was balanced. It was all about the mix, Lowe told himself, and right now his recipe was near perfect: caffeine matched against the jet lag, pint of milk against the burning patch in his gut, reefer and John Jameson against the coke and those pills that Margot gave him. It teetered on a knife edge, and Lowe knew that it could get away fast—but not just now. Now, in the best part, he was riding an exquisite soap bubble—drifting, warm and light, through a damasked, luxury-suite landscape. He looked up and saw Margot's hair in blue-black curls around her pale face. Her robe fell open and he saw her small, round breasts, still pink from the shower. He stretched his legs on the sofa. Sex had rubbed him raw and he settled himself gingerly and closed his eyes.

Besides the weightlessness and Margot's slender thighs under his head, Lowe's favorite part of the best part was the disconnection. Balanced this way, past and future held no dread and he could reflect on both with serene detachment.

He reached up and dragged a lazy hand across Margot's breasts. She batted him away and picked up a fashion magazine. Lowe smiled to himself. Floating in his bubble, even Margot didn't scare him much. He could think about their time together calmly now, without the dizzying mash of lust and fear she'd filled him with almost from the start. Christ, was it only ten weeks since personnel had sent her?

It was January but she'd been bare-legged. Her calves were white and shiny, and the little tattoo on her ankle was penny-green. Lowe thought it was a bruise at first, but it turned out to be some kind of braided cross. She'd worn a black leather coat that day, and her black hair tumbled past the collar. Something about her 1980s do and her slanted eyes and the way she talked reminded Lowe of Sheena Easton— though he didn't know if Sheena Easton's eyes were blue like Margot's, or if their accents were the same. They weren't.

That was a hellish month in the back-office—a new computer system, the trading room churning out twice the usual number of deals, and half his staff out with flu—but Margot had pulled her weight and then some. He remembered how quick she was reconciling payments, and how accurate. The other clerks didn't like her much but there was no question she knew her shit. After a day or two they were following her lead, and so—in his way—was Lowe.

She was like a tune stuck in his head, and all of a sudden his morning train ran too slow and the workday went too fast. Overtime was a gift and he relished every second, down even to the lousy takeout meals—anything that got him alone with her, and got him close enough to smell whatever made her smell so good.

When he was close, he couldn't stop looking. He was cautious at first—careful not to stare—but as time went by his eyes grew hungrier. If she noticed, or minded, Margot gave no sign, and after a while Lowe didn't give a damn. He pored over her from follicles to fingernails, and memorized every inch. Once, late on a Thursday, he'd had to stop himself from touching. He left her in his office and walked the halls and wondered what his forty-eight-year-old brain was thinking. Looking was one thing, he told himself, but his palm on that white calf . . . By comparison, the talking seemed so harmless.

Drifting, Lowe smiled at the thought. How long before she'd known all about him—ten days, maybe? Two weeks? From his high school varsity letters and his dropping out of b-school, to his twenty years at the bank and his promotion, five years ago, to manager of the back-office—he'd told her everything. To which she'd nodded and looked into his eyes and said next to nothing about herself.

Not that Margot was the silent type. When it came to crude humor she held her own with the other clerks. She toned it down a little for him: some deferential teasing— subtle flattery, really; jokes about the size of the trades they were processing—how any one of them would make a nice lottery prize; and, inevitably, her favorite game—*what if*. What if you could go anywhere . . . do anything . . . start all over again? What if you knew then what you know now? What if you won the lottery?

Her daydreams were of travel—first class all the way. "And none of this nature shite, thank you—it's cities only. Trees are fer parks, and animals fer zoos or eating."

Lowe's fantasies were more modest, but Margot coaxed him along.

"Would've gone easy on the pitching in middle school—saved my arm for later.

"Wouldn't have majored in accounting.

"Would've traveled more—London maybe, or Paris."

And then, on another Thursday, she'd coaxed him far-ther. Even as the words left his mouth, Lowe knew there was no going back.

"I wouldn't have married so young, I guess . . . or maybe not at all." His face burned and his eyes bored into the car-pet. Margot didn't answer, but when he looked up she was staring at him.

From his bubble, Lowe could see that sex was inevitable after that. Which isn't to say that he wasn't surprised when it happened, or that he didn't nearly burst an artery when he saw that hard white body for the first time. A word had popped into his head then, something from high school English—what was it?

It was a Tuesday and there were accounts to balance and Lowe thought she'd be working late. He was surprised when she appeared in his doorway at 5:00, coat on her arm.

"I'm through those accounts and if there's nothing else, I'm off," she said. Disappointment hit him like a sandbag. Margot looked at him and at her watch. "You want a coffee before I go?" she asked. It blunted his upset a little and he nodded. But when they got to Water Street, Margot headed not for Starbucks but for a taxi. Lowe followed.

"There's a place uptown you'll like," she said, and she said nothing else for the rest of the ride. The place was a sleek hotel in Murray Hill, where the desk clerks dressed bet-ter than Lowe. They nodded at Margot as she crossed the lobby. The room was large, and Margot kept the lamps off and opened the drapes and let the city light in. She pulled her shirt over her head and stepped out of her shoes and skirt.

"Look all you like now, Jimmy," she whispered. "Fer as long as you like." *Alabaster*. That was the word.

Her body was limber and smooth in a way that his wife's had never been, even before the kids. Every time was better than the time before, and every time left him gasping and starving for more. The mattress was on the floor when they came up for air. Margot hit the minibar and brought back tumblers of John Jamesons. Lowe hadn't been quite sober since.

Things moved quickly after that. Margot whispered in his ear—talk of *what if* and *lottery tickets*. She had it all worked out, and she had a friend in Europe—a Mr. Flynn—who knew useful things like how to launder money and how to get new passports. She made it sound so simple. One trade, identical to thousands of others in the system, except that it was fake. But there'd be nothing fake about the payment the system would wire out.

"Dead simple," she'd said, and she was right.

Leaving his family was easier than he'd expected, too—at least at first. As images of Margot filled his head, his wife and daughters had faded to grainy silhouettes. Audrey was barely a shadow when he told her about his business trip. So was his boss when he put in for vacation. Dead simple.

Margot had booked the flights. They'd gone first class to Brussels. She told Lowe to lay off the booze and drink lots of water but he didn't listen. His head was splitting when they arrived and things had been hazy ever since—a blur of swank hotel rooms and rainy cityscapes and never quite knowing the time. Zurich, Amsterdam, Luxembourg, Frankfurt—and in each, a friend of the unseen Mr. Flynn, with papers to be signed. They all knew Margot, but it was Lowe's signature they needed. Lowe had worried about the documents, and the nameless men, and Flynn—wherever he was—and he'd wondered about Margot's hotel room in New York, and the other hotels, and who was paying. But the questions always stumbled from his head before he could ask them, and Margot was there to put a pen in his hand, and afterward a drink and her hard white body.

Somewhere—Amsterdam maybe—Lowe's stomach had started to burn, and he found himself thinking of his family. It was incoherent stuff—vague worry about . . . he wasn't sure what—but the thoughts left him empty and aching. Three times he'd mentioned them to Margot, and not again.

The first time, her lower lip had trembled. "I thought I made you happy," she'd said softly. Then they fucked until the sheets were drenched.

The second time went less well. "I'm not yer feckin' priest," she'd snapped.

The third time was in Frankfurt and her voice made him jump. "Jaysus—enough with yer feckin' regrets! It's over and done but you poke at it like a bad tooth." She shook her head. "Yer pretty feckin' Irish for a New York Jew, Jimmy—you'll fit right in in Dublin." Ten days in the city now and he still didn't know what she'd meant.

Not that he'd seen much of Dublin besides their hotel room. Waiting for Flynn and their passports, Margot grew steadily edgier. She was restless and paranoid—stir-crazy, but reluctant to leave the hotel. It was only because he had started to annoy her, Lowe knew, that she allowed him his walks each day, to the park and back. He wondered what she was worried about, and what would happen when they got the passports. Would Margot go with him to another city? Did he care? The thought of not having sex with her made Lowe sad, and the thought of traveling alone scared him, but in his bubble he didn't dwell on these things long. Margot leafed through her magazine and perfume fell from the pages onto him. She shifted her hips and Lowe thought about the body beneath her robe and reached for her again. She was having none of it.

"Yer head's too heavy," she said, and slid off the sofa. She went to the window and looked down on the gray city and the gray Liffey. Lowe felt his tranquil bubble burst and his balance slip away. He opened his unwilling eyes.

"What time is it?" he asked.

"Time fer yer walk."

He nodded and a large liquid weight shifted in his skull. She was right, he thought, his head was too heavy, and over-full with booze and static—a pail of mud on a rickety perch. Lowe rubbed his eyes. He pulled on clothes and slipped two midget whiskey bottles into his raincoat pocket. He looked at Margot. She was still by the window with her head against the glass.

Though Margot had told him not to, he took the same route to the park each day. The buildings he passed were mostly low and old, which made the new ones look even taller and glossier. The streets were full of young people who looked like bankers and accountants and computer guys, and looked like they'd come from someplace else. It reminded Lowe of Wall Street that way. Maybe that's what Margot meant about fitting in.

He took a wide, tree-lined avenue deep into Phoenix Park, to a bench by the pond he'd been staring at all week. The air was damp and burrowing cold, and he shivered when he sat. The park was mostly empty now—old people, dog walkers, a couple strolling down the path. The woman had thick red hair and an umbrella. The man was tall and pale and his hair was pitch black. Lowe had seen them in the park before and wondered if they worked nearby. He closed his eyes and listened to birds and distant cars and the crunch of footsteps on the gravel. He opened his eyes when the footsteps stopped.

It was the couple, looking down at him. They were handsome, Lowe thought, though there was something cold in the man's lean face, and something angry in the woman's eyes.

"May I?" the man asked. American.

"Help yourself," Lowe said. The man sat; the woman remained standing and looked up and down the path. "You from the States?" Lowe asked.

The man nodded. "From New York, Jimmy—like you."

Lowe wasn't conscious of trying to get up, but suddenly the man's hand was on his shoulder, pressing him back. Lowe's mind raced, but without traction.

"Relax, Jimmy," the man said.

Lowe's mouth went dry and the rest of him was bathed in sudden sweat. "Flynn?" he asked finally. The man reached into his coat pocket and pulled out five photos and laid them on the bench.

"She brought them to Dublin, Jimmy, same as you," he said, pointing at the photos as he spoke. "And Dublin's the last stop." He said some names but Lowe had trouble hearing him. A roar filled his ears as he looked at the pictures of the five dead men, and suddenly he couldn't see. He must've been leaving again because the man had him by the arm and the woman looked worried.

"Five, in five years," the man said. "You make it half-a-dozen."

Lowe slumped on the bench. "Flynn?" he said again. It was an old man's voice.

The woman shook her head in disgust. "There's no Flynn but herself—Kathryn Margot Flynn."

Lowe gripped the little bottles in his pocket and looked at the ground. "You're cops?"

"She is," the man said, nodding at the redhead. "I'm private, working for your employers. The good news is they just want their money back. You make that happen, and keep your mouth shut, and they won't prosecute."

Lowe clawed at his gut. "What's the bad news?"

The redhead looked down. "I am," she said. "I don't care fer yer girl leaving bodies all over my city, but I got no proof of anything. That's where you come in."

Lowe slumped on the bench. He opened his mouth to speak but nothing came out. He looked at his hands and saw the little whiskey bottles in them. He cracked the metal cap on one and the man took his arm.

"Let's wait on that, Jimmy," he said, but Lowe shook him off and drank one bottle and then another. The woman spoke, but Lowe couldn't make out the words. His head was down and his eyes were closed. He was waiting for his balance and another bubble to ride, but in his heart he knew it was no good. The best part was over.

# THE GHOST OF RORY GALLAGHER
## BY JIM FUSILLI

He'd left London in disgrace. A banking scandal, one of the worst. More than a half-billion pounds sterling in losses, bolloxed up every trade he made for months, going deeper and deeper. The end of days for the 230-year-old Ravenscroft Bank. Hundreds sacked. Pensions gone. Dreams shattered. Suicides, at least five of them, including Desmond Chick, for thirty-eight years the janitor at the Con Colbert Street branch in Limerick, a widower, raised three sons himself, working dusk till dawn. Sent away without so much as a plaque for comfort, he cried himself to death, they say, too old to start anew and as heartsick as if he'd lost his Minnie all over again.

The trader, meanwhile, was sentenced to four and a half years. Got out in three. Good behavior, though the arrogant shite never owned up to what he'd done. Eleven hundred days in Coldbath Fields and every one spent planning to cash in like Nick Leeson did—a book, Ewan McGregor on the silver screen, lectures—his reward for breaking the Barings Bank in '95. Now you can play poker online with Leeson, punters thinking, Here's yer guy, he'll ride a bad patch straight to hell.

None of that for this trader, save a photo that went on the wires: scowling, bruised, itching, hollow eyes darting this way and that, maybe two stone lost to labor. No publishers, no producers; banking scandals old news now, a story already told. His wife gone off with an orthodontist, moved to Hamburg. Not even a word from his mot Trudi, tossed aside by the *Sun* after she told of their life together, all coke and cognac, laughing at regulators and the likes of Desmond Chick before they tracked him down.

Ah, Trudi, bleached-blond and beyond plump, a hostess now at the Odyssey in Bristol, and she knows her time has passed. Her fifteen minutes and all. Let the Remy warm her belly and she'll talk the ear off a man's head, give him something she never told them at the *Sun*. Ever hear about the only time he expressed regret? No? Well, Ducky, we were in that big comfy bed of his in that hotel in Tokyo, and he props up on his elbows, and he says, *Trudi, they can keep it all, the bastards. Every last piece, every last shilling. But I'll tell you, I'd give my left thumb to have back my old guitar.* That being what they call a white-on-white 1961 Fender Stratocaster. Owned and played by Rory Gallagher, it was. Rory Gallagher, love. Sure, you heard of him. Rory—*Rory Gallagher,* for fuck's sake . . .

As for the trader, the bitter prick, still thinking who he was, packed up and disappeared. Did a good job of it too. Four years gone by now, and not a word. Man barely qualifies as a bit of trivia these days.

Funny, isn't it? Sometimes, when the world is turning and the craic is good, it almost seems as if it had never happened.

The trader, clever man, reemerged in Dublin, just another stranger brought in on the wave of the Celtic Tiger. Had a plan, he did: shaved his head, and when his auburn hair grew back he done it blond and spiked. Put 80,000 miles on the Audi, nose redone in Nice, jaw in Seville. Teeth in Milan.

Didn't have to do much about the accent. Born in Sligo, he was, not London, as he claimed.

As for wardrobe: gone were the Spencer Hart suits, Turnbull & Asser shirts, Hermès ties, Fratelli Rossetti shoes. Would've run around like Kevin Rowland, scruffy Dexy himself, *Come on, Eileen*, if he could've, if it wouldn't have drawn eyes. Instead, old jeans, T-shirts, a gray Aran sweater, and a brown knit, and he put holes in the elbows with a Biro, having tossed the Parker Duofold. (Not true: Like all else, the fountain pen was seized and sold at auction.)

Figured now he could hide in plain sight, more or less.

With all the expenses, he still had about 300,000 euros stashed here and there. No one knew, not even Trudi.

Decided to buy himself a perch and look down on the world, laugh as the rabble passed by. But then it came to him: no, he wanted his nose in it, wanted to smell the stench of ordinary life, to listen to the love song of the forlorn, revel in their petty grievances, in their miseries, watch as the bloody stasis took hold, watch as the light dimmed and died.

The trader bought himself a pub.

A dump over on the north side of the Liffey, off the Royal Canal, a regular shitehole it was, a right kip. Entrance in a stone alley beyond mounds of rubbish, and you couldn't stumble upon it without a map. Celtic Tiger, my arse, it seemed to say. Two steps down and the rainwater flooded the drain, and that was all right too. Mold and rotten wood, the floorboards sagging.

The place reeked of failure, of resignation.

Perfect.

"Welcome home, you bastard," the trader said as he stepped over the moat, dusted his hands, coughed.

It needed a name, didn't it?

The trader, who by now was calling himself Eamonn or English Bill, depending, thought about it, and his first instinct was to call it "Rory's." No, "Ballyshannon," after Rory's birthplace. "The Calling Card," that's a good one, after Rory's—

"I must be out of me feckin' mind," said English Bill to no one.

Which wasn't far from true now, was it? Talking to shadows, the cobwebs: took more than one roundhouse to the side of the head in the community shower in Coldbath Fields, he did, though well short of what he had coming.

Pitch black now in the pub and he doesn't know it, maybe his eyes have gone weak again. Thinking a little crank would do him good.

"The Rag and Bone," he said, his throat feeling like he ate sand. Thinking of his childhood, and Yeats.

Yeah, and soon tour buses are parking out front and the Japs are snapping photos, thinking they've tripped over history.

Back to square one, and two hours later, still not a clue. And then another hour after that, come and gone.

Cheesed off, he came up with "Póg Mo Thóin," as in "Kiss My Arse," but he let it float, and he fell asleep on the bar, woke up to the gnawing and *cheep-cheep* chatter of a rat inches from his skull.

Got up, pissed in the sink when the jax was two feet away. Cupped his hand and took a mouthful of brown water, felt the rust wash over his Italian teeth.

Soon, sunrise and thin white light through the veins in the painted windows, and he can see the booths against the mud-brick walls, drunk-tilted and ready to fall in on themselves, creaking even in the shouting silence, and who'd give a shite?

And then, like inspiration, like Yeats dreaming, "Cathleen Ni Houlihan," it comes to him: "Desmond's."

Brilliant.

But he don't know why.

"Desmond's," and he likes the sound of it. "Desmond's." Likes it because it don't mean nothing.

They started coming within minutes after the Guinness and Murphy's trucks pulled out, smelling it as they stumbled along, squat little men, and they were the dregs and had nothing to say. The same story, again, again: never had a break, this bastard or that, she was hell on earth she was; ah, but me dear sweet mother, I'll tell ya, and me da, Fecky the Ninth he was, but, God, I loved him. Sitting but a stool apart, three, four of them, each brutalizing the same tune. Clay faces in the flicker of cheap candles, a motley bunch straight out of Beckett, and moths flew up from under their tattered greatcoats.

The trader wanted entertainment, stories of the long, long fall, and soon he realized he had put Desmond's at the end of the shite funnel, and who but them was going to appear?

"Jaysus," he said as he rinsed a glass in foul water, "the sin of pride, my arse."

"What's that you say, Eamonn?" asked one of the sagging men, spider veins, rheumy eyes, fingers stained piss-yellow, paralytic before noon.

"I said, 'Get the fuck out.' All of you." Shouting, bringing it from the bellows. "You and you and you!" Finger stabbing the air, and there's the door. "Out! O. U. T."

The men shrugged, plopped down, hitched up their trousers, and slouched out, forearms a shield from the sun.

And then the trader made a mistake.

He jammed the bolt across the door, poured himself a pint to wash the crystal meth off the back of his throat, went into a threadbare carton, and dug out Rory's *BBC Sessions*, cut in '74 but released when he was in Coldbath Fields, four years after Rory died. Whipsnap "Calling Card," "Used to Be" like a cold knife against yer spin. The trader blasted it, oh did he blast it, and they heard it in the alley through the cracks, the ancient splinter wood, rattling bricks. The trader had every piece of music by Rory Gallagher that was ever recorded—all the officials, bootlegs too, bits of tape, third-generation copies; snatches of solos, rehearsals, sound checks, Rory turning the white Strat into a chainsaw, Rory levitating.

The bastards didn't get the trader's stash when they sent him up, the pricks, they let his lawyers cart it away; and he could tell you which was the solo in "Walk on Hot Coals" on *Irish Tour '74* and which was the night before, two nights hence, thanks to some boyo who smuggled in a recorder under his coat. The trader had twenty-one versions of Rory doing "Messin' with the Kid," one more kick-ass than the next, and he blasted every one of them, and more, for four days and nights straight, shaking Desmond's to its foundation.

And when he opened the door, they were lined up halfway to the Liffey, shivering in the cold, shuffling, frozen fingers tucked under their arms. Hopeful eyes now. Expectations.

Word was a Rory pub was opening by the Royal Canal, and they wanted in. Rory was their man. Rory pushed the blood through their veins, and if someone was going to pay him tribute, they were going to be there, ice and snow and wind and hunger be damned.

"What the fuck?" the trader said, squinting against the silver light, suddenly wishing he hadn't the need for more crank and something other than stale crisps.

By 8 o'clock they were three deep at the bar, totally jammers, and the snug was swollen, and Rory wailed, setting the fingerboard ablaze, and the trader had hired himself a bouncer and a lass to clear the tables. The next day he needed a man to pull the taps, and a plumber to fix the jax.

By the time he closed on Saturday night, he'd netted 1,100 euros on nothing but beer and Rory. The guy from the chipper round the block offered him a stake, saying business tripled since Desmond's was born, thinking he's on to the new Temple Bar. The Black Mariah pulled up, the Gardaí came in, and the trader prepared to slip them a gift, "Sinner Boy" pounding the walls and all, but they loved Rory too and as long as no one lit up a fag and the coppers got in, Desmond's was sweet, at least for now.

"Jaysus," the trader said as he made a neat stack of his notes, "the whole country's full of eejits."

He folded the bills, crammed them in his pocket, and was thinking he'd found justice. Finally, he told himself, he was getting his due.

He did the lass on the cold floor, ripping her from behind, and she went home in tears, mascara running down her baby cheeks.

A week or so later, past closing time, but the little pink man in far booth stayed glued to the wood, though the power had been cut and the votive candles gave little light.

The bouncer was in the alley, tossing them off cobblestone, so the trader, his ears ringing, went across the beer-soaked boards.

"Thinking of moving in, are ya?"

The little pink man reached into his coat and placed an ergo machine on the tabletop.

The trader blew onto his hands, the chill returning now that the crowd was gone.

Suddenly, a piercing note from a Stratocaster split the air, followed by a blinding flurry that knocked the trader to his heels.

The music continued for almost four minutes, burning ice daggers, an angel blasting pure light. Pinwheels, butterflies, blood spatter on virgin walls. Grace.

Neither moved, the little pink man starting intently at his enraptured host.

"Where'd you get it?" the stunned trader asked when silence returned.

"It" being a Rory he'd never heard.

Little Pink Man eased back toward the brick.

"Well?" the trader repeated. The crystal meth had him pumping nitro, bugs crawling on his lungs, and yet it had been Rory, beyond doubt.

In a small, eerie voice, Little Pink said, "We call him up, is what we do."

The trader frowned, scratched the top of his head. "Listen, just what's your game—"

"We call him up and up he comes," Little Pink repeated. "Now, for someone like yourself, that is all and more. A mystery, true. But all and more, is it not?"

The trader couldn't focus to study the visitor, there in his too-big hound's tooth, his black tie pulled tight to his pink neck. Nose a ball of putty, a hint of an impish smile.

Little Pink reached with a translucent finger, popped open the machine and pointed to a silver disk much smaller than a standard CD. Candlelight skittered across its surface.

"Take it," Little Pink said as he wriggled out of the snug. "Take it and know there's more."

The top of the man's head, covered in curly red hair, sat below the chin of the trader, who had snatched up the disk as if it were the gold of Mag Sleacht.

"Who are you?" His accent slipped, revealing his years far from home.

Little Pink turned up his coat's collar, the darkness carrying a chill. "I'm the man who's knowing how to bring you to Rory, I am."

The trader watched as the little man leaped the moat and vanished.

A moment later, the bouncer, whizz-wired like his boss, said he hadn't seen a little pink man, no, Eamonn, why? And if you don't mind, I'll be on me way . . .

"Lock it behind ya," the trader said, turning his back.

Pitch black save the light of the player, cranked to the gills he was, listening over and over and over to the guitar solo until near dawn, the hair on the back of his neck up, *Rory, Rory,* and the trader knew whatever the little pink man wanted he'd get. All of it, the hidden 300,000 euros, the money in the till, the money yet to be made. Desmond's, if need be. All of it.

All. Of. It.


It took four days for Little Pink to return, four unbearable days, and he brought Fat Pink with him. They stood in the doorway on the business side of the moat, deadpan and composed.

The trader saw seraphs, and he tried to turn off the frenzy in his mind and under his skin.

The bouncer, dim bastard, held them back, being it was

past midnight, and the trader had to scramble across the room to halt their dismissal, freezing the dope with an X-ray stare as he grabbed Little Pink by the forearm.

"Come," he said, almost desperately, "come."

They went to the little office he'd fashioned out of the storage room.

"Jaysus, where have you been?"

"It'll cost you," Fat Pink said, his voice a throaty growl.

"Huh?"

"What me brother is saying is that the ghost appears at no charge, but we have our expenses," said Little Pink, collar up on the hound's tooth.

He saw they had not a mind for charity.

"Sure," said the trader. "Expenses."

The Pinks kept still.

The trader took a breath. "Go on."

"We all get what we pay for," Little Pink said. "In the end, the accounts tally."

And with that, the trader had found his hitching post. Negotiations had begun.

"But you've seen this place," he said. "Be flattery to call it a dump."

Big Pink looked askance at the beam an inch or so from his head. The cobwebs had cobwebs, and the wood wore moss.

"Suit yourself," Little Pink said, with a faint shrug.

The visitors spun slowly toward the door.

"No, no. No," said the trader, groping again for Little Pink and to hell with negotiating. "What I'm saying is I don't know what I can raise."

"Sure you do." Fat Pink said it.

Little Pink dipped into his pocket: the machine, the button, and this time it was Rory on the twelve-string acoustic guitar, a slow, agonizing, gorgeous blues. No singing, not yet, but pain released from deep in the heart of Ireland filled the musty room. The sweet chirping of blackbirds too, and platinum rain, and yer ma's tears.

"Oh," the trader moaned. "Oh, sweet Jaysus."

The music stopped when Little Pink popped open the device.

He held out the disk. A gift, and Fat Pink didn't mind.

"Recorded not twenty-four hours ago," said the little man.

The trader swallowed hard. "Name your price."

They settled on 75,000 euros—Little Pink knowing the U.S. dollar was weak—and the Audi. In return, they'd record for as long as the ghost chose to play.

Driving in the rain through Ballsbridge toward Kill o' the Grange, headlights sweeping across the diamonded windscreen, the trader had it figured. He'd report the Audi stolen before he left Stillorgan Road for the meeting, record Rory, glorious Rory, and then he'd double-back on foot to grab his money, putting the sight of the bouncer's Ruger MK right between Fat Pink's googly eyes.

He'd pick up a new set of wheels in Spain and be in Seville by tomorrow noon.

That was fair play to the boys in Coldbath Fields, and he wasn't too far gone with the beatings and the crank to have forgotten what he'd learned in the yard. A real tutorial it was, day in and out.

The call made, he put the mobile back in his pocket, and rolled down the window, searching for a sniff of Dublin Bay. None, his nose as numb as stone.

"Eejits," he said to the night air. "Eejits and wankers. Come to rip off Eamonn the barkeep, and look who's here. The man who broke the Ravenscroft."

He was still chattering when Fat Pink opened the door to the cottage on a grainy road two rights and a left off Kill Avenue, and there's yer open field and the black tree branches groping for the indigo sky.

"You're early," Fat Pink said, filling the door frame, all but blocking out the light.

"I got the money."

The rustle of wings, or his imagination, all too alive.

"Well?" said the trader, who'd left the Ruger in the glove box.

Fat Pink stepped aside.

The wobbly stairwell was his only choice, and he all but leapt from his head when Fat Pink killed the lights.

"What the—"

"Whisht now," Fat Pink warned as he joined him on the creaking stairs. "Remember what we're on about."

"I can't see," the trader mumbled. He stopped at the landing, wondering where to go. As his eyes began to adjust, he saw a white knob and started for the door in front of him, but Fat Pink grabbed his shoulder and led him along the banister.

The floor creaked too. The house 200 years old if a day.

And in the room, gaslight.

Little Pink and another guy, bulldog snarl, neck as thick as a post, his melon flat on top.

"This him?" Pug asked.

Little Pink nodded.

The trader squinted and he saw an old table, longer than it was wide, and two chairs. The fireplace had been shuttered awhile ago, and the green shades on the windows were drawn.

Fat Pink nudged him in.

"How do we do this?" the trader said, his voice cracking. Darting bees xylophoned his ribs, the march of wind-up ants, barbed wire made of licorice and lace.

Pug took a sip from a half-pint, offered it to no one.

"We wait," Little Pink replied. He pointed to a chair.

The trader walked in, and the trader sat down.

Fat Pink took the chair to his left. The flickering gaslight made his features quaver and dance.

Leaning against the slate mantle, Pug twisted his head until his neck cracked.

As if anticipating the question, Little Pink said, "Hours, minutes. You never can tell." He took out his silver machine, set it on the table.

"That's what you're using? No microphones? You've got no facilities?"

Pug grunted and Fat Pink pushed down a laugh.

"It's what we use."

Dumb bastards, the trader thought. You get the ghost in a recording studio and you're John Dorrences, you are.

He folded his hands on the table, and Fat Pink turned round to Pug, but neither man spoke.

Skeleton key in hand, Little Pink locked the door.


Five minutes later, felt like five hours, the trader sat tall when he heard the snap-squeal of an electric guitar going into its amp, and a quick punch on the strings to make sure it was in tune.

"Calm yerself," Fat Pink said.

Little Pink nodded toward the machine.

And soon the sound of a Fender Stratocaster filled the room, and the ghost was running his blues scales, warming up, and soon he was toying with some old Muddy Waters lick, and the trader knew his man was working his way to something brilliant. And then the guitar let out a cry and a hole in the sky opened and here it came, lightning and molten gold and, God in heaven, it was glorious.

The trader shut his eyes in bliss.

And Fat Pink grabbed him by the left forearm and wrist, pressing the man's hand flat on the table, and with one brutal swoop of a hatchet, Pug took off the trader's thumb.

Blood spurted, and it ran in a river toward the machine.

The trader howled and the trader howled, and he was almost as loud as the guitar, the blizzard of blues notes, the screeching feedback, the beauty.

Pug took off his belt, wrapped it around the trader's left arm, cutting the flow.

Standing, Fat Pink put his hands on his shoulders, pressed the trader deep and hard into the chair.

Little Pink, off the door and tapped the machine. Silence. Absolute silence, save a man's agony cry.

"And you had to name it after him, didn't ya?" Little Pink said, glaring at the trader, his eyes colder than cold.

Pug was digging in the trader's pocket for the Audi's keys.

"Desmond's," Little Pink went on. "That's your idea of a joke?"

The trader's thumb lay on the table, pointing with recrimination at its former host.

"I don't—Jaysus, my hand. Look at my—"

Little Pink smacked him, and then Little Pink smacked him again.

"My name is Chick," he said through grit teeth. "His name is Chick, and the man going to your car is named Chick. We're from Limerick, and we don't forget."

"I don't know . . ." Near shock, the trader blubbered and whimpered. "My thumb . . ."

"Our father was a good and decent man who didn't deserve to die 'cause of the likes of you."

Despite the searing pain, the trader was starting to get it. Ravenscroft, and some people won and some lost, but who the fuck is Chick?

Little Pink stepped back and he smiled, and when he smiled, Fat Pink smiled too.

It was Fat Pink—Larry Chick being his real name—who came across Trudi in Bristol, and it was Bernie Chick—him the one the trader dubbed Pug—who heard about the guitar player over in the States in Red Bank, New Jersey, who could play it like Rory done. Little Pink, who was Paul but went by the name Des to honor his father, put it together. The club off the Royal Canal was a gift, it was. The crystal meth situation too, meaning the trader didn't think to see if Bernie was behind him when he finally stumbled back to his ratty flat.

"We're going to take your teeth too," Des Chick said.

"And the nose," Larry nodded.

"And the nose," Des agreed, "if Bernie comes back empty-handed."

The trader could not believe he had been duped. Better than them all, and smarter, and yet he'd been duped.

Des said, "And then we'll talk about regret."

The trader looked at his thumb on the table, and he heard the one he called Pug trudging up the creaking stairs.

# LOST IN DUBLIN
## BY JASON STARR

Kathy had come to Dublin to forget about her fiancé, Jim, or to at least reassess the relationship, but so far she hadn't been able to stop thinking about him. She'd called him twice—once, minutes after her flight landed, under the pretense of wanting to find out how Sammy, their year-old Labrador, was doing, but it was really to hear *his* voice; and again when she arrived at the hotel to admit that she missed him. He said he missed her too and told her that this was crazy, to get on the next plane back to New York, but she told him no, she had to stay, to try to "work this thing out once and for all."

Now, as she lay in bed in the curtain-darkened hotel room, trying to sleep off her jet lag, she wondered what the hell she was doing with her life. For years, all her friends had been trying to convince her to dump Jim, and part of her wanted to do it. She knew she'd never be able to trust him again—for all she knew, he was back in bed with that bitch right now—so what was the point in even thinking about staying with him? But it had never been easy for her to let go of things and she'd been with Jim for six years, and although things had been stormy, to say the least, she felt she had to at least give it a chance—see if there was still something there.

She stirred for a couple of hours and then got up, not sure if she had slept or not. She still had a bad headache and felt out of it, and a shower and a whole small bottle of Killarney sparkling from the minibar didn't help. But she was excited to go out exploring and she figured a good cup of coffee would perk her up.

She picked up a tourist map and went down Chatham Street to a pleasant-looking café and sat at one of the tables outside. A waitress came out and asked her what she was having.

"Just a coffee," Kathy said.

The waitress left and Kathy opened the map and was very confused. Dublin was a maze of streets with Irish names and she had no idea where she was. It didn't help that she had a lousy sense of direction. Normally when she traveled she relied on Jim to take her from place to place. Jim was one of those guys who seemed to have a compass implanted in his brain and always got a handle on a city instantly, even if he'd never been there before. The last trip they'd taken together was to Paris, two years ago, and she never looked at a map the entire ten days. Jim whisked her around the city, from *arrondissement* to *arrondissement*—walking to some places, taking the Metro to others—and she never had to worry about anything.

The waitress brought the coffee. Kathy had a sip, then noticed a guy at the table next to hers smiling at her. She hadn't noticed him before and she figured he must've sat down while she was looking at the map. He was working on a laptop and was kind of cute.

She smiled back at him and then he said, "You're American, are you?"

Kathy felt a wave of guilt she experienced whenever she was traveling and was outed for being American, as if her nationality was something to be ashamed of and kept hidden when abroad.

"I guess that's pretty obvious, huh?"

"The map and the accent were sort of giveaways, I suppose. Hi, I'm Patrick, by the way."

"Hi, I'm Kathy."

He asked her if it was her first time in Dublin. She told him it was, and that she'd come because her father was born here and she'd always wanted to see it. When she told him she was from New York he said, "Ah, love New York. I was there once when I was at university, but I want to go again. I'm a playwright, you see."

"Really?"

"Well, aspiring. Had one play produced last year, at a small theater here in Dublin."

"That's great."

"Believe me—it sounds more impressive than it is. The theater's a twenty-five-seater and it was empty half the run . . . Are you on holiday with your husband?"

Kathy saw Patrick looking at her engagement ring.

"Oh, no," Kathy said. "I'm not married . . . I'm not even sure I'm engaged anymore, actually."

"So you're here with friends, are you?"

"No, I'm here by myself, actually."

"Oh, that's very nice. If you need any suggestions on places to go, I'd be delighted to help out."

"Actually, if you could tell me how to get to the O'Connell Street area that would be great."

Patrick came over and circled O'Connell on Kathy's map, and marked several other spots, writing in the names of his favorite restaurants and pubs. Kathy liked smelling Patrick's cologne and it felt good with him close to her.

After a few more minutes of pleasant small talk, Kathy looked at her watch and said, "I better ask for my check and get going."

"Would you mind doing me a small favor?" Patrick said. "Could you watch my laptop for just one minute?"

"Oh, yeah," Kathy said. "Sure."

Patrick smiled—he had nice dimples—then went into the café. Kathy caught the waitress' attention and made a scribbling motion with her hand. The waitress nodded but was busy taking another order.

Kathy looked at the map, at the markings Patrick had made, thinking how nice he was for doing that. He was kind of cute and he had a sexy accent. Too bad he was too young for her—he seemed to be about twenty-two or twenty-three—and she never really liked artsy-type guys.

She was looking closely at the map, at the location of a good produce market which Patrick had circled, when it happened. She was aware of someone moving quickly next to her and then she looked back and saw the guy with dark wavy hair sprinting away down the block. Instinctively, she grabbed her purse, relieved that it was still there. Then she looked back at the guy who was running away and realized he was holding Patrick's laptop.

Kathy hesitated and didn't say anything for a few seconds, until the thief had already turned the corner, and then she screamed, "Stop him! Somebody stop him!"

The waitress and a customer—a man in a business suit—came out of the café.

"What happened?" the waitress asked.

"Somebody stole a laptop," Kathy said.

"Where'd he go?" the man asked.

"He just ran away . . . around the corner," Kathy said. "Can't you call the police or something?"

Then Patrick came out and seemed confused. "What happened?"

"Your laptop was stolen," Kathy said.

Patrick peered at his empty table with a look of horror, shock, and disbelief.

"I'm so sorry," Kathy said. "This guy just came down the block and grabbed it."

"Did you see what he looked like?" the man in the suit asked.

"No," Kathy said. "I just saw him from the back . . . He had wavy hair. He was wearing jeans."

"I don't think that'll help the Gardaí very much," the waitress said.

"Go ahead and call," Kathy said. "Maybe they can catch the guy."

"I'll call," the man in the suit said, and he took out his cell phone and walked away.

Patrick was sitting, devastated, with his forehead against the table.

"I'm so sorry," Kathy repeated. "I don't know what to say."

"I had everything on that machine and it wasn't backed up," Patrick said. "My whole new play—it's gone."

"I feel so awful," Kathy said. "I mean, the guy came up so quickly. I didn't even see him."

"Maybe they'll catch him," the waitress said.

"Bollocks they will," Patrick said, looking up. His eyes were red and teary. "The cops never catch those fuckers."

"It's my fault," Kathy said.

"Why's it your fault?" Patrick said. "This city's going to shit, I'm telling you. Bastards."

The man in the suit returned and said, "The Gardaí will be here soon."

"Not soon enough, I'm afraid," Patrick said.

"You never know," Kathy said. "Maybe they'll catch the guy."

"Yeah, I'm sure they'll try really hard to find a laptop," Patrick said.

"Yeah, it's doubtful they'll catch him," the waitress said.

"I don't know what to say," Kathy said. "I feel responsible."

"What do you mean?" Patrick said.

"You asked me to watch it and I didn't. I got distracted. It's my fault, I guess."

"I don't know what I'll do," Patrick said. "It took me a year to save up for that computer. And they cost a lot here—much more than in America."

"I'm really sorry," Kathy said. "Wait, I know." She reached into her purse. "Let me give you some money."

"Don't bother," Patrick said.

"No, it was my fault—here." She dug into her purse. "This is all the cash I have—here, take it." She handed Patrick some bills. She wasn't sure exactly how much was there, but she'd exchanged $200 into euros at the airport.

"Really, I appreciate the offer," Patrick said, "but it's not necessary."

"Please, you have to," Kathy said. "I feel awful."

"I'm not taking your money."

"You have to. Come on, I know it's not enough for a new laptop, but it'll have to help. It'll make me feel so much better if you took it."

"It's really not necessary," Patrick said. "It took me two years to save up for this and I can save up again. Until then, it's back to pen and paper, I suppose."

The waitress shook her head and went away to take someone's order.

"Good luck," the man in the suit said, and he went back into the café.

"I guess the Gardaí'll be here soon," Patrick said to Kathy. "You don't have to wait."

Kathy was still holding the money. She was starting to cry. "You have to take the money," she said. "If you don't, I won't be able to stop thinking about it my whole trip and I'll have a horrible time. Please, just take it."

Patrick looked away for a few moments then turned back and said, "I suppose if you're insisting . . ."

Kathy gave Patrick the money. She apologized a few more times then just wanted to get away. She took her map, then went into the café to charge the bill on her AmEx since she didn't have any more cash. When she returned Patrick was still waiting for the police, wiping tears from his cheeks.

"I really am sorry," Kathy said.

"It's all right," Patrick replied. "Have a great time in Dublin, all right?"

"I'll try to."

Kathy walked away, relieved. Following Patrick's instructions, she ambled along Grafton Street and across the Hapenny Bridge. Still shaken up, she wasn't able to absorb much of the city. For a couple of hours, she just wandered around, window shopping, figuring she'd do the real touristy stuff tomorrow. She was hungry and went to one of the restaurants that Patrick had suggested—an excellent Thai place on Andrew Street. Surprisingly, she didn't feel at all awkward or self-conscious sitting at a table alone and she didn't miss Jim at all. She had a couple of glasses of wine with dinner and got a little drunk. When she left the restaurant, she passed a cyber café and decided to just get it the hell over with already. She logged onto her e-mail account and wrote Jim a note.

Jim,

I'm sick of this bullshit. You're a liar and you hurt me so bad and I just can't pretend anymore. You can keep the apartment—I don't care anymore. But I'm taking Sammy and the leather love seat. I'll pick up the rest of my stuff when I get back to the city. And don't forget, YOU caused this, not me. YOU fucked up!!

Goodbye (for good this time!!!!!)

Kathy

She clicked *send*, logged off, and left the café. She felt great, like she'd definitely done the right thing. She'd taken too much of Jim's crap for too long and it was time to move on. She knew her friends would be proud of her.

On her way back to her hotel, she was tempted to stop for a drink at a trendy-, fun-looking pub, but figured she'd be better off getting a good night's sleep and a fresh start tomorrow.

A friendly older man was working at the hotel's front desk. When he gave Kathy the key to her room, he asked her how she was enjoying her stay in Dublin. Kathy told him she liked the city and then told him about the incident with the stolen laptop. When she got to the part about how awful she'd felt and how she'd offered to give Patrick money, the man at the desk said, "Jaysus, you didn't give him the money, did you?"

"Yeah," Kathy said. "Actually, I did."

"I was afraid of that. You fell for a scam, I'm afraid."

"A scam?" She had no idea what he was talking about.

"Was there another man there, besides the one who lost the laptop?"

"What do you mean?"

"They work in a team of three. One has the laptop, one steals it, and one comes over to help. Is that what happened?"

Remembering the guy in the suit who'd offered to call the police, Kathy said, "Yeah, there were three guys, I guess. But I really think you have it all wrong. This guy's laptop really was stolen."

Kathy went on, explaining what had happened, but the man at the desk cut her off and said, "I'm telling you, love, it's happened before and we were even talking about warning our guests about it."

"I don't think you understand," Kathy said, recognizing the anger and frustration in her voice because she was starting to realize what had happened but didn't want to admit it to herself yet. "This guy went to the bathroom and someone else—a stranger—came running down the block and—"

"It wasn't a stranger," the man at the desk said. "They were working a scam. They must've picked you out as a tourist. Were you holding a camera or a map or something that made you stand out as a foreigner?"

Kathy couldn't believe she'd let this happen to her.

"Yeah, actually, I was."

"Jaysus, it's awful this happened to you. You didn't give him a lot of money, did you?"

"No," Kathy lied. "Just ten dollars . . . I mean euros."

"Well, that's a blessing," the man said. "This retired couple from Florida gave them a thousand euros because they felt bad for the guy. I'll tell you one thing, though—that guy must be a good actor. I mean, to get people to believe him—that takes some talent."

"Well, good night," Kathy said, and started away.

"Should I call the Gardaí?"

"No, that's okay. It was only ten euro."

"But the Gardaí should really know about this so they can—"

"I really don't want you to call . . . but thank you."

In her room, Kathy tried to forget about the whole thing. There was nothing she could do about it now and she definitely didn't want to get into a whole thing with the police—answering questions, maybe even having to go to a precinct or wherever. It was better just to forget about it—pretend it hadn't happened.

She washed up and got into bed. She'd bought a few thick paperbacks to read during the trip, but she wasn't in the mood. She turned on the TV and flipped around, but there was nothing to watch except soccer and news. She was watching the BBC News reports about the latest violence in the Middle East, though she was thinking about Patrick. He'd seemed like such a nice young guy—so charming and helpful—but that should've been a warning sign. The whole thing was such an obvious setup, the way the thief had appeared out of nowhere to grab the laptop and then how that guy with the business suit came right over to help, and of course it was *he* who'd offered to call the police. She was angry at herself for falling for that crap, for being such a victim. In New York, there was no way something like this would have happened to her. In New York, she always had her guard up and was naturally suspicious of everyone. If someone started talking to her at a Starbucks in New York she would've said a few words to him and ignored him. And in New York she never would've been so vulnerable. She was traveling alone for the first time in a foreign city and she was preoccupied with a lot of personal things. They'd probably zeroed in on her as a perfect victim.

In the glare of the BBC news, Kathy had a long, hard,

self-hating cry, and when she finally recovered she missed Jim. Yeah, he'd cheated on her and, yeah, he'd treated her like shit, but he was a good guy and she loved him. She felt safe and protected and secure when they were together. Without him she was lost.

Kathy couldn't believe she'd sent that e-mail; that had to be the stupidest thing she'd done today—much stupider than falling for the scam.

It was about 5:30, New York time. She tried Jim's cell and their home number, but there was no answer. She kept trying, off and on, for the next few hours; he either wasn't home or was screening calls. Then she realized that, since she'd written to Jim on their AOL account, she could "unsend" the message if he hadn't read it yet.

She went down to the front desk, waited for the man to finish a phone conversation, and then asked him if there was a computer with Internet access she could use.

"I'm afraid the business room is closed," he said.

"This is an emergency," she said. "I have to e-mail my fiancé."

"I'm terribly sorry, but the door is locked and I don't have the key. The guy who does have the key should be back in about a half hour though."

"What about your computer?"

"I'm afraid it's not connected to the Internet."

"Is there an Internet café close by?"

The man gave her instructions to one that was open twenty-four hours a day.

Kathy raced out of the hotel and, after a couple of wrong turns, found the café, which was still very active. She had to wait a few minutes for a computer to become available. It was past 9 o'clock in New York and Kathy didn't see how Jim couldn't be home by now. He always checked his e-mail first thing after he came into the apartment, so it seemed impossible that this would work.

It was a slow connection, but she was finally able to log onto AOL. Kathy opened her "sent mail" file, clicked "unsend" on her message to Jim, and discovered that the message hadn't been read yet.

"Thank God," she said aloud as she unsent it.

Later, back in her hotel room, she called Jim and he picked up on the first ring. He explained that his cell battery had died and he'd been out wining and dining a client. Kathy sensed that he was lying, that he'd really been out with that bitch from his office again, and that he might've even brought her back to the apartment with him. Still, it was a relief to hear his voice, to know that everything would return to normal, and she said, "God, I miss you so much, sweetie. This is the last time I go anywhere without you."

# TAINTED GOODS
BY CHARLIE STELLA

A broad tells you you're a comfortable fit, what it means, make no mistake about it, boyos, it means you have a small dick, she's trying not to hurt your feelings," Jack Dugan said.

Dugan was a tall gangly man of fifty-two years. He had a thinning hairline, a long uneven nose, and dark deep-set eyes. He was dressed in a black polo shirt, black slacks, and black leather loafers. He wore thick jewelry on his wrist and around his neck. He'd been drinking since the early afternoon. Now that he'd switched to the hard stuff, he was rambling in overdrive.

"It's the same thing, you hear about a broad has a nice personality," he went on. "Maybe she does, maybe she doesn't. You're guaran-fuckin-teed, though, she has this great personality, she's no looker. Comfortable fit is the same fuckin' thing. It means you don't need to stand around a locker room full of Mandingos to know you were robbed at birth. It means you're the type has to crowd the piss stalls. Even the stalls in this place, which are like fuckin' showers, you got a comfortable fitting dick, you don't want nobody else to see it. Not that they can that easy, anyway."

The two men sitting across the table were twin brothers from Ireland several years younger than Dugan. Both were stocky men of five-foot-ten; each weighed about two hundred pounds, had short blond hair, blue eyes, and thick necks. The older of the twins by a few minutes sat directly across from Dugan. He had grown a fuzzy blond mustache. He played with it from time to time.

"Now, take that missy over there, the kid from Dublin," Dugan continued. He pointed to a slender waitress carrying a tray of drinks away from the bar. "Nice bright smile, the red hair, the freckles, the green eyes. Pretty girl, no? Not the type you'd turn away it comes to bedding down for the night. Her, you don't give a fuck about her personality. It isn't the thing. Her, you feed her whatever it takes to get her pants down. She's a looker, plain and simple. No feelings to hurt, once you've done the deed."

Dugan belched into a fist before downing a shot of Jameson. He slapped the glass down and reached for the half-filled Bud bottle on the table. He took a quick drink from the bottle and belched again, this time loudly.

"Excuse," he said.

Dugan wiped sweat from his forehead with the back of his right hand and then pointed at the twins, one at a time.

"You want a shot, just say so. Don't be shy, boyos."

The twins had pints in front of them. They waved the offer off. Dugan poured himself another shot of Jameson.

"Here's a little tidbit about that one, the missy I just mentioned," he said, and then pointed at the same waitress again. She was setting drinks on coasters at a round table with a party of six. "She likes it in the ass, that one. Purrs like a fuckin' cat, you set the anchor there."

The twins turned to take a better look at the waitress. They were both smiling when they faced Dugan again.

"And the thing is," he continued, "the best thing, she's a little off in the head, if you understand what I'm saying." He wiggled a thumb alongside his right ear. "Some kind of condition from shock, the poor thing was taken by a crew busted out of Mountjoy, took turns with her until she was soft as shite. Gangbanged for two days until the Gardaí found them. Her head's fucked ever since."

Dugan stopped as the twins turned again to look at the girl.

"Catherine, her name is," Dugan said. "Catherine Collins." He leaned forward to whisper. "Call her Cathy, you're petting her head while she polishes your knob. She likes that. Purrs, I swear to God."

He stopped to take another drink from the Bud bottle.

"Comes across a little retarded, like she can't think for herself, but she can, don't kid yourself. She asked for it there, her brown spot. Turned and pointed."

The twins smiled at one another.

"She was tainted goods, why they shipped her here," Dugan went on. "Whatever those cons did to her, she's taken a shine to being a pin cushion. Auntie Mary back home can't keep watch while she's running her bar on the north side. Catherine come over under the eye of the ape bouncer here, Rusty. Have you met him yet? He's not here tonight, but he'll pick her up after closing. Big fucker. Him you don't wanna mess with. Not even the two a'you."

Dugan yawned before he continued, "He's some kind of relative, Rusty is. Her cousin, I think. He's a cunt hair less daft than the girl, but he can lift trees out the fuckin' ground, he gets angry enough. Snapped an Italian's arm off the end of the bar one night for giving the same missy some shit and grabbing her ass."

Dugan was watching the girl now.

"Shame it is, too," he said, "an ass like that going to waste."

He wiped one side of his mouth on his shoulder. The waitress Dugan was talking about stopped at their table to pick up an empty bottle.

"Thanks, hon," Dugan said. "You're looking very pretty tonight."

The waitress smiled at all three men and moved on.

Dugan was about to go on when a well-dressed couple distracted him across the room. He stopped to watch a fat, middle-aged man with an attractive, well-dressed older woman. They were seated at a table and immediately attended to by another waitress.

"There he is," Dugan told the twins. "Don't look. He's directly behind the two of you. First table off the stairway."

The twins looked down at the table.

"I'd like to take the fat fuck and throw him down the stairs," Dugan said. "Take his wife downstairs to the kitchen and fuck her in the ass on the chopping board, make him watch."

"How do you want us to handle it?" the older brother asked. His accent was thick.

Dugan suddenly smiled in the direction of the couple. He spoke without moving his lips. "She's a flirt, the cunt he's with. Nancy, her name is. Likes to cock tease. Likes to do the halfway thing. I've had her down in the card room more than a couple times. She seems to think it's okay I jam three fingers up her twat, she gives me a blowjob afterward. That isn't cheating to her. Never let me fuck her, though. Not yet. She'll suck your dick till you're dry, but she won't let you between her legs with it. I guess that's keeping the marriage vows sacred enough. Who'm I to argue?"

He waved at the woman.

"The cigar nights they have in this place," he continued.

"Our man brings her along for sport. She flirts with every guy in the joint while he's getting tanked. Then she takes a few too many trips to the bathroom, if you know what I mean. Likes to reaffirm herself, I think."

The twins were eyeing her husband.

"I'm here, I find my way downstairs with her myself," Dugan said. "I don't know that he knows or not, what she's doing down there all that time, but he doesn't show it up here. Up here, most the time, he watches her like a hawk. Unless, of course, he's on the hustle, which he is a lot more often lately, he can't pay his bets."

Dugan took a long, deep breath. He seemed to forget where he was in the story. The eldest twin leaned forward, motioning toward the man Dugan had been talking about.

Dugan pointed a finger between both twins and picked up where he had left off. "Then, when he's trying to squeeze somebody for some bullshit investment in his government contract bullshit, his attention is focused on whoever the mark is. Usually, another well-dressed guy can't hold his liquor. Like the sucker owns the Irish joint on First Avenue, Donahue's. A nice guy, Alex. He took it up the ass for thirty grand from this fat fuck. I heard, I told the guy, gimme half the note. I'll hang that fat slob out a window until he scams somebody else for the thirty grand he owes. I'll hang him an extra few minutes for a few more on top of the thirty, teach the deadbeat a lesson. Or I'll take my cut and be very happy with that, fifteen dimes. That's the only time this slob is focused, though, when he's on the make for new money to bet with. Otherwise, he's a very jealous fat slob cocksucker."

Dugan held up his beer to toast the couple across the room. "I don't get her angle, though," he whispered. "Tell you the truth, why she's with him, I don't get that at all. She's up there herself and all, maybe fifty, fifty-five or so, but she can do better than him. She has to know his story. He's on the edge of the cliff with more than one office taking bets."

Dugan returned his attention to the twins. "Ryan no longer has the patience to wait this prick out. And I need the scratch now so I can bring it to Dublin and keep the boyos off my back. There's five hundred in it for you two, to make an example of this scam artist. His number has come and gone, far as I'm concerned."

The brothers nodded.

"I heard you," Dugan said. He was smiling at the woman across the room again. "How do I want you to handle this? I'll follow herself down when she goes to the powder room. I'll keep her down there longer than usual. I'll hold her fuckin' head in the toilet, I gotta. He'll eventually go down to see what's the problem. You'll follow him. The card room is straight ahead once you're in the hall with the ladies' room. Take him in there, deadbolt the door behind you, gag him, and break his face. Leave him tied so he can't move until somebody from the place finds him after hours."

The brothers nodded in unison.

"And make it ugly," Dugan said.

Six days later, Dugan woke up in a damp basement on the north side of Dublin. A hard-looking slender woman in her late forties put fire to a cigarette across the room. She wore a stained kitchen apron and boots. A stocky man puffing on a pipe sat at a table off to the right. His face was unfamiliar to Dugan.

"He's coming around," the woman said.

Dugan strained to see her. He'd been drugged upstairs in the bar the night before after passing off money from Marty Ryan to three IRA soldiers. They kept him drinking from a

Jameson bottle spiked with poteen. Dugan had nearly poisoned himself from drinking.

The woman was sharpening a boning knife at a table near the stairway. Dugan struggled to see clearly. It hurt to hold his head up for long.

He remembered drinking in the men's room with the soldiers. He remembered them slapping his back and telling him jokes. He remembered laughing out loud and passing the bottle.

Now he couldn't remember much of anything else.

He had come to Ireland with the twins because Marty Ryan had told him it was important they travel together. Dugan remembered sitting next to them on the flight over. He remembered joking with them. He remembered going through customs together and taking the cab from the airport.

They had separated once they were in the bar, Dugan going off to the men's room with the soldiers while the twins drank at a table. Dugan couldn't remember when they had left or where they had gone. He couldn't remember leaving the men's room.

He knew he was on Gardiner Street because the cab had dropped them off in front of the bar. Dugan remembered thinking the old neighborhood always looked the same and that he was glad to be done with it.

A door slammed shut somewhere upstairs. "That'll be him," the woman said.

Dugan was feeling cramped in the shoulders. He tried to move from the chair and realized his hands were tied behind his back.

"What's this?" he muttered.

A door opened at the top of the stairs. The woman gave a nod at the stocky man.

Dugan thought he recognized the woman. "Mary?" he said.

She didn't flinch.

Dugan looked to his left and saw a blue plastic tarpaulin covering something on the floor. He belched and could taste vomit. He gagged from the taste.

There were heavy footsteps on the stairs. Dugan looked up toward the sound. The woman pulled a string cord and a bright light filled the room. Dugan turned his head from the light.

He heard whispers. He tried to open his eyes and felt himself slipping back into unconsciousness.

He was back on the flight with the twins. They were joking about being with the girl, Catherine, the night after Dugan had told them about her. They had stopped by to chat her up and learned her cousin had left early. She had cab fare to get home, but they gave her a lift instead.

"She went without question," one of the twins had told Dugan. "Like we were sent from heaven saving her six bucks."

"We spent the night taking turns," the other twin had bragged. "First me, then Sean, then me again. This way, that way. She finally cried when she was fecked raw around sun-up. We did save her the cab fare, though. And you were right, until she cried, she purred like a feckin' kitty cat."

Dugan remembered telling them, "I told you so."

"Sorry I'm late," Dugan heard a deep voice say. He opened his eyes and saw a hulking shadow at the foot of the stairs.

The huge man had a thick red beard and looked familiar. He leaned over the woman and kissed her forehead.

"Rusty?" Dugan said. "What's going on? Why am I tied?"

"You're to answer for Catherine," the woman said.

Dugan was confused. "Catherine?"

"My niece."

"Mary?" Dugan said. "Mary Collins."

The woman took a drag from her cigarette.

"I'd've liked to be here earlier," the big man said.

"The soldier boyos took care of it," the woman said. "They were happy to help."

Dugan saw she was still holding the long sleek boning knife. "What's the knife for, Mary?"

"You," the big man replied.

"But it's easier when the bones are popped from their joints first," the woman said. "Why I waited for Rusty here. He caught a late flight."

Dugan turned to the big man. "Rusty, what the hell is this? What's going on?"

"The other two had something to offer, the boyos took mercy and shot them in the head," the woman said. "Cutting them up afterwards isn't a problem. It's only when you're keeping them alive so they can feel it does it make a difference. That's when it helps, the bones are popped or pulled from their joints first."

The big man grabbed one end of the blue tarpaulin and whipped it off of two dead bodies. Dugan saw it was the twins laying across one another. He saw a hole in the back of one head before he saw the one with the mustache had been shot through the eyes. Dugan gagged twice before he was sick on himself.

The woman was standing now, holding the boning knife in one hand. She held a pint of Guinness in the other. She sipped from the pint before handing it off to the big man.

"Oh, God have mercy!" Dugan whimpered. "God have mercy."

"Those two talked about what they did to my niece after they had too much to drink," the woman said. "The wankers went back to the bar and told it to the wife of the man they beat for you and Marty Ryan, thought they could double-team her, too, from the shite you'd said about her. They tried to feck with her head, told her they'd beat her husband again unless she did what they wanted. They weren't very bright, the twins. It all got back to Rusty here. From the woman herself. Nancy, is it?"

Dugan was shaking his head.

"The boyos here saw the knife and gave you up in a flat second," she added. "Everything you told them, how we sent her off because she was tainted, you fucking shite. You didn't have a clue, but you felt like talking, eh?"

"It's what I was told," Dugan said. "I swear it, Mary. I was told she'd been raped by felons from Mountjoy and lost her mind from it."

"She was," the woman said. "And she was affected, but we sent her away so she'd never have to hear the name of the place again. Never have to see it."

"I'm sorry," Dugan cried. "I'm sorry, Mary."

"Herself asked for permission to bring you back here," the big man said. "Or you'd've been killed in New York. Marty Ryan offered to take you out himself."

"It was only once," Dugan pleaded. "Just the one time, I swear. I was pissed. I was fuckin' berco."

"Well, you're tainted now," the big man responded.

The woman said, "The question is, you feckin' piece of shite, is will you purr like a cat when Rusty pulls your bones from their joints, or will you wait until I cut you to feckin' pieces?"

# PART III

HEART OF THE OLD COUNTRY

# WRONG 'EM, BOYO

BY RAY BANKS

W elcome to Dublin, sir."
"Get tae fuck."
It was an hour from Edinburgh to Dublin, all cramped up in the belly of a Ryanair with attendants who didn't bother to show us the escape doors. One of 'em had the pure blarney shite running free from his puss. I could tell he was a poof, likes. Graham Norton type, y'ken?

Then the cunt of a cab driver, same old shite. A leprechaun with fuckin' eyebrows on his cheeks. He skinned us out of most of my funny money and dropped us off on O'Connell Street. Best Western, the Dublin Royal. I wondered how royal a three-star could be, got my answer when I saw my room: not fuckin' very. I dumped the Head bag and switched on the telly. Couple of channels, they wasn't even speaking fuckin' English. I lit a Bensons and cracked open the bottle of duty free. Jack Daniel's. Took a swallie and put the bottle on the bedside cabinet. Looked out of the window, felt sick. Call this culture? Princes Street, that's culture. This is a motorway with a couple of fuckin' statues of nobodies.

This country, man. I'd been here before, but that was thirty years ago. Hiding behind a wall in Belfast, trying not to shite my uniform. I had a gun then, mind. Thanks to yer man Bin Laden, the best I could manage this time was a Stanley the Big Yin give us when I was sixteen.

Big Yin. His name was Connolly, like the other Big Yin.

And if the comedian had carried on drinking and being funny instead of marrying that blond piece, he'd have looked like our Big Yin too. Must admit, I fancied a wee shot at her when she was in that leotard in *Superman 3*, likes, but when I found out she was a head-shrinker, Wee Shug wilted.

Big Yin was the reason I was here. Him and a mick called Barry Phelan. A bunch of old scores to be settled and me buff apart from the Stanley.

It didn't matter. A solid blade was all a Boyo needed.

Walking with Big Yin, him finding his feet slow. We was going down the chipper on Broughton Road. He had a winter coat on and his breath came out in short blasts of smoke. Ice on the pavement and I had to guide him over it.

"You got a name for us, Shuggie?" he said.

"Aye. Barry Phelan."

"Away, I thought he was dried up."

"That's what I heard, Mr. Connolly. A man with a gun in his mouth doesn't lie."

"Good lad."

I got the name from Lee Cafferty, a bristling big-fuck suedehead who'd been the leader of a gang of sawn-offs. This bunch of pricks had turned over a card game behind one of Big Yin's massage-and-handjob places down London Road. And for a hard cunt, Cafferty was quick to piss his tartan boxers. Mind you, when you thumb back the hammer of a revolver, it's like St. Peter slammed the book shut. Sorry, auld son, Big Cat says y'ain't coming up.

"What d'you want done?" I said to Big Yin.

He coughed, shook his head. After he cleared his throat, he said: "I want the cunt deid is what I want, Shugs. Bastard thinks he can jump the pond and do over one of my places?"

Big Yin pulled a face. His cheeks went hollow and in the glow of the streetlamp I could see right through the skin. "I want his balls. You do that for us, son. You go over there and you bring us back his fuckin' balls while they're still bleeding."

"Okay."

We went into the chipper. Big Yin got a poke of chips drowned in vinegar. About the only thing he could taste. He told the plooky lass behind the counter to keep the change and I escorted him out. The wind coming strong up the hill, I had to hold onto Big Yin's arm as we went back to his house. He struggled with the chips, dropped a couple. I got him back home, took off his coat, and got him settled in his chair.

"You want a nightcap, Mr. Connolly?" I said.

"I widnae say no, Shugs."

Poured him a double-dram of Glenlivet and sat the glass on the table next to him. He turned on the telly and caught the beginning of a *Minder* repeat. When I left, I could hear him humming the theme tune.

That night, I sat in the dark because my eyes hurt. I tanned a bottle of brandy, listened to Johnny Cash, and held the Stanley Big Yin had given us. I didn't need light to know what was on there. My finger traced it out: "*Shuggie BTTE*"

Boyo To The End.

Aye, that'd be right. I slipped the Stanley into my pocket, went to pack my bag.

"You're kidding us, you're fuckin' *kidding* us."

"Honest, Shuggie. I widnae kid yez around on this, man."

"You couldn't have telt us before I got on the fuckin' plane? Jesus Christ, man."

"I didnae get a chance, Shugs. I only found out this morning. You got a black tie?"

"Fuck yersel'," I said, and slammed the receiver back on the cradle. Missed, slammed it again. I could still hear Keith whining at the other end. Smacked the phone so hard, the speaker part came off in my hand. Left it at that and saw a young mick punk waiting to use the phone. Said, "Fuck you staring at?"

"You what?" he said.

I walked over to him. "How do I get to Mount Jerome?"

"You get him drunk enough, he'll do anything." The punk rolled his shoulders, reckoned hisself a piece of work with the nose ring and that stud in his eyebrow.

"Fuck's that, eh? Irish sense of humor?" I grabbed the fucker by the arm, hauled him into the phone box. Pressed him up against the glass. "How's about a Scottish joke, then? This smart cunt's got no nose. How does he smell?"

"Wait a second—"

"He fuckin' doesn't." I pulled the nose ring out, took the nostril with it. He tried to clap his hand over the ragged wound, but I held him fast.

"Hey, hey, hey," he said. "I'm just kidding around, man."

"Stuff it up your arse. Tell us where the fuckin' cemetery is or I'll pan yer cunt in."

"You get the bus from up the road," he said. When he talked, he spat.

"Which one?"

"Sixteen. Get off at Harold's Cross."

I pushed him to the floor of the box. Pulled my hood up and wandered across the road to the bus shelter. Lit a Bensons, watched the white part get spotted with rain. The punk found his feet and took off. Run, Forrest, run.

Barry Phelan. Some radge bastard had already done the job for me, and His name was God. A stroke knocked Phelan into the Beaumont and a heart attack finished him off in the wee small hours. A shock for all concerned. Mostly me. And if I could take the Big Cat to task, I fuckin' would. Just like Him to cheat a trying man, ken what I mean?

My man Keith was supposed to keep his ear to the ground. He was supposed to tell us where Phelan was when I got here. I'll sort him out before I go. Useless fucker. Wouldn't be surprised he got hisself hooked up with the wrong crowd, ken? It was getting that way. People didn't have respect for tradition no more.

The Bensons tasted rank. I chucked it into a puddle as I saw the bus coming.

What's the difference between an Irish wedding and an Irish funeral?

One less drunk.

Aye, I'm a funny cunt. And I needed something to lighten my mood when I got to Mount Jerome. The place was a sea of gray, man. Tombstones, creepy bastard crypts and whatsit . . . *mausoleums*? An Irish funeral in the middle of a cloudburst. Talk about fuckin' maudlin. I walked through the stones, making sure I trod on as many of they dead cunts' heads as I could, sidled up against a tomb, and watched all they bastards in their drookit Sunday best watching God's lad go through the motions.

Ashes to ashes. Funk to funky.

The mourners, they was mostly family. I could tell because they was ugly bastards. Skinny, suits hanging off them like they was three sizes too big. The women, small and stodgy, hidden away behind tatty black veils. Professional fuckin' widows, ken? And it pished down throughout. I spat at the ground, put my hand in my pocket, and wrapped my fingers around the Stanley.

Barry Phelan's balls, they was under that screwed-down lid. Unless I shot over there, jumped on the coffin, and pried it open with my bare hands, Phelan's balls were going to be worm food along with the rest of him. That wasn't any big deal. Bollocks was bollocks. There was bound to be another lad round here who I could pass off as the real deal. And I saw him as soon as the coffin went under.

He came to me, hand outstretched. A tall lad with a gut and white hair. "Tommy Phelan."

I shook. His hand like a wet fish supper in my grip. I read somewhere that a man's scrotum and nose kept growing as he got older. If that was the case, then this Tommy Phelan must've had knackers the size of watermelons, I'm telling you, because that nose made him look part toucan. "Hugh Sutton," I said. "Mates call us Shug."

"You're Scottish," he said.

And you're a fuckin' genius. "Aye, fae Edinburgh, likes," I said, getting coarse with the cunt. He wanted Scottish, he'd get Scottish. "I heard Barry kicked it, likes, so I thought I'd mosey over and check it out."

"You knew him?"

"I ken Lee Cafferty."

"Lee's a good man."

Lee's a dead man. I shot him in the crown, left him sticking to the lino like a fly in shite. "He certainly is."

"You'll be coming to the wake," said Tommy. A statement.

"No can do. Got to be back in Edinburgh."

"Sure, you can stay for a wee while. I'd be offended if you didn't."

"Ach, if you put it like that," I said, "I'd be glad to."

* * *

An Irish wake, like a Scottish wedding, Hogmanay and Burns Night all rolled into one. A cold spread on a long table up against one wall that'd hardly been touched. Empty bottles that had. We was upstairs in this place called The Lantern. Phelan sitting across from us, a half-tanned bottle of Bushmills and a pint of Guinness next to it. Talk about fuckin' stereotypes, man, the auld lad was half in his cups and two sheets to the wind about an hour after we got there. He had a Players between his fingers. I didn't ken they still made 'em.

"What do you think of Dublin?" he asked me. But like most soused micks, he didn't wait for an answer. His face screwed up and he leaned forward, rattling the table. The black stuff didn't move. "It's not Ireland," he said. "It's England's *version* of Ireland. You know you can't smoke in pubs over here now? Legislated. We're losing our culture bit by bit."

"Aye." Thinking, *Smoking's part of your culture, pal?*

"Sure, you know all about that, don't you? I been to Edinburgh, I seen what they did to that place. Shops on Princes Street all full of See-You-Jimmy wigs, am I right? Fuckin' English screwing you out of your heritage. Tourist tat. Am I right?"

"Aye, you're right."

"Dublin's the same. Temple Bar, I was down there the other week, it's full of coffee shops. *Theme* pubs. Feckin' yanks coming over here claiming they have ancestors from the feckin' bogs. You know what I say? I say *feisigh do thóin féin,* that's what I say."

"Gesundheit," I said.

A young lad came over to the table. He was stringy, had

a mean look about him. He put a bottle of clear liquid on the table and Phelan's eyes lit up like a cheap fruit machine. "Now that's more like it. You'll join me, so."

"I'm all right, Mr. Phelan."

"My brother died, the name's Tommy, and you'll join me. Won't he, Barry?"

"Course he will," said the stringy lad. He took a seat. I knew he was a wanker, because he turned the chair and straddled it.

"My nephew's just come back from your neck of the woods," said Tommy. He poured three deep shots from the bottle. "Barry, this is Shug. He's an Edinburgh lad."

"Pleased to meet you," he said. But his eyes said different. His index finger ran down the side of the shot glass. Brown flecks under the nail. "It's done, Tommy."

"There's a good lad. You take care of it yourself?"

Barry looked across at me, like he was trying to work out if it was safe. Then: "The auld bastard was dead when I got there." He cracked a grin like a graveyard. "Fucker was sitting in front of the telly, Tommy. Sitting in his own shite."

I smiled. My mouth was open. Some fuck had put vinegar on the roof and it hurt to breathe. I reached for the shot glass. "What's this, vodka?"

Tommy's face flickered. "*Poitín*, Shuggie. *Sláinte*."

"*Sláinte*," said Barry.

"Whatever," I said, and necked it. It burned my throat. That, or something else.

A rat always knows when he's in with weasels. That's the way the song goes.

I drank with them, tried to hold it down. Kept wanting to twitch right out of there. Barry didn't drink so much, and neither did I, but Tommy got wasted. His eyes glazed over, his chin got loose. It looked like he was melting. "Your da would be proud of you, Barry-son. He'd be *proud*."

"I know, Uncle Tommy."

Barry Phelan, son of Barry Phelan. The fuckin' Irish, they keep it simple, eh? They have to, the amount they pour down their necks. I got a measure of Barry right away. This cunt clocked on who I was, likes. That's why he told me what happened to Big Yin. Laughing at me. It tore at my gut, made me want to chew his fuckin' nose off.

Shug Sutton. The last of the Boyos. The rest all up and fucked off with other firms. Shuggie stayed put. More fool me, eh?

I waited until Barry got to his feet and announced that he had to take a pish. Waited another three seconds and did the same thing. Tommy out of it. I walked into the toilets and Barry had his back to me, pishing in one of the cubicles. Too insecure to use the urinal, hung like a fuckin' hamster, eh?

"I don't hear pissing, Shugs," said Barry, shaking his wee man. Took more than three shakes, the wanker. "Which means you're thinking about doing something rash, am I right?"

I didn't say anything. Couldn't find the breath.

Barry turned in the cubicle. He smiled. His bottom set of teeth was all skew-whiff, likes. "Yer man's dead, Shugs. He was dead before I got there. So you go back out there and you raise a glass to the new crew, all right? Because if you don't, I'll have the whole family rip you a new arse to match yer fuckin' face."

I thought about that for about five seconds. And the cunt Phelan made to push past me. I stood still.

"You fuckin' simple, Shugs? It's over, pal," he said.

Right enough. It was over.

I clamped a hand over his mouth, grabbed his balls with the other, and pushed him back into his cubicle. His breath was hot on my palm. I cracked his skull against the wall until he went limp. Lost myself for a second, then came back with blood on my hands and saltwater hanging from my mouth. My lungs hurt. I couldn't breathe proper.

Slapped the lock across the cubicle door and let Barry's head drop against the toilet bowl. Fumbled for my Stanley and pulled the cunt's drawers down. Wiped my nose with the back of my hand and sniffed hard, slumped down onto the floor with him. Got to work. Had to keep wiping my face because I couldn't see through the water.

Outside I heard people singing country songs. Cunts didn't cry at the funeral, but stick on Patsy Cline and they greeted like bairns.

"Crazy." Of all the fuckin' things to hear.

I leaned back against the toilet, mopped my face with my sleeve. The cunt had bled all over the shop, the tiles sticky. And there was me, sitting right in the middle of it, man. Britches all fuckin' bloody and that, my shirt a mess. It stank of Barry's last pish and blood and shite. I let my head fall back and I stared at the lightbulb hanging from the ceiling, red dots in front of my eyes.

Barry Phelan didn't kill Big Yin; God did. And it didn't matter which Barry Phelan did the London Road blag, didn't matter that Big Yin wouldn't give a fuck if I had the cunt's balls or not.

I promised him, ken? You can't go back on a promise to a dying man. Especially when you was all the poor bastard had.

And aye, there was no way I was getting out of here alive. If I'd had that gun I put Lee to the lino with, I'd have had a fighting chance. But right then, my arse wet through with Barry Phelan's blood, I didn't have the strength in me to do fuckall but sit there and listen to Patsy fuckin' Cline and Tammy fuckin' Wynette, tears rolling down my cheeks.

Took they cunts an hour to realize Barry was a no-show. Took another fifteen or so to check the bogs. And daft fuckin' micks, took them a bucketload of mouth and one hard kick to bust down the door.

I heard a lad puke. Heard the hammer of a revolver thumbed back and oaths yelled, proper nasty Irish shite.

It's not every day a lad admits he died with another man's balls in his hand. But what else was I going to do, eh?

I was a Boyo to the end.

# THE PISS-STAINED CZECH
BY OLEN STEINHAUER

T his was back in '94, in the middle of a planned three-month stay in Prague. I thought that by soaking up a little Bohemia and wading through Joyce's *Ulysses*, I'd become a writer. But that was a joke, largely because I spent each night drinking with Toman, a six-foot shaved-bald Czech who passed his days in the gym. He liked buying drinks for a writer, and I liked having drinks bought for me.

"You come to Dublin on this weekend."

"I don't know. I've got to work."

"A *writer's* work," he said, puffing out his chest like a Cossack, "is to living. Only one night. Weekend. You come."

"I'm broke, Toman."

He slapped my back. "We stay with Toman's friend, Sean. The plane—Toman will pay."

"You have a friend in Dublin?"

"Toman, he has friend all over world!"

He liked referring to himself in the third person. *Toman must to pee*, or *Toman must get to work*. I never knew what his work was, but he had enough money to keep me in drinks, which was all that mattered.

We landed at Dublin International on January 22, a Saturday, then took a taxi to a posh southern neighborhood called Ballsbridge—a name that got a giggle out of me—where the bay winds blew down a narrow street of matching brick Victorian houses. It was very fucking cold. The door Toman knocked on was opened by a skinny Irishman with a beard that made me think of the drunks lingering in the corners of pubs in *Ulysses*—everything I knew about Dublin came from that book.

"Shite. Toman."

"Toman and his American writer friend are here for until tomorrow. You have a floor?"

I was embarrassed, because we clearly weren't expected. All I could do was introduce myself as Sean reluctantly led us inside.

"How is our Linda?" asked Toman.

"Gave her the boot. You know." Sean took a green bottle of Becherovka, the Czech national liquor, from a cabinet. It was the last thing I expected to drink in Dublin. He handed me a shot. "Whaddaya write?"

"Trying to write like Joyce."

He raised an eyebrow, his expression not unlike scorn.

So I said, "How do you know Toman?"

Sean lipped his glass, then poured it down and wiped his mouth. "Real estate investments. In Prague. Toman, he helps me out. He's the go-between."

"Toman helps," said Toman, "so my good friend Sean can buy all of Prague for his friends."

"What friends?" I asked.

But the Irishman didn't hear me. "A pint, lads?"

A pint, it turned out, meant ten pints in three pubs—the Paddy Cullens hidden in the embassy area; Crowes a few doors down; and by 11:00 I was dizzy in Bellamy's, where at this hour all the surfaces were sticky and rugby boys were singing to each other and businessmen at the bar swapped jokes over Guinness. Toman and Sean drained their Harps and roared over jokes about Linda-who'd-gotten-the-boot ("*Och, ochón,*" said Sean, "she had an ass onner!") and others whose names I couldn't keep track of. They liked my Zagreb drinking stories from five years before, where after finishing most of a bottle, we'd pour vodka on the dorm floor and set it alight or spark a match at the mouth of a bottle and watch it shoot, rocket-like, down the corridor.

Toman preferred the ones about running into Zagreb police at 3 a.m. This was still during the Communist times, but my Croat friends would drunkenly yell at the militiamen, calling them idiots and just daring them to arrest us. "I don't know why we didn't end up behind bars."

"Because they know it is true," said Toman. "Police, they are idiots."

"The Gardaí wouldn't arrest you," said Sean, wiping Harp from his wet beard. "They'd bust your head, strip ya starkers, and toss ya in the Liffey, ne'er to be heard from again." He shook his head. "I'm pissed."

We watched him get up and stumble to the toilet.

Toman leaned close with the atrocious breath that would often portend a shift into Czech seriousness. "Olen, you want to be writer?"

I was drunk enough to answer with soulfulness. I placed a hand on his shoulder. "Toman, my friend, a writer is the only thing I want to be."

"True?"

"Absolutely."

"Then come," he said as he stood up.

On his feet Toman was steady, but I wasn't. "Where we going?"

"Toman helps you become writer."

"Dandy," I muttered.

He led me to the bathroom, and through the alcohol I became hazily worried, but for the wrong reason.

"Not all writers are queer, Toman."

He didn't answer as he pushed through the door. It was empty save for Sean, who was trying to focus his wobbly stream into a urinal. He noticed us. "Aye, I'm *óltach*."

That was another thing I didn't understand. Later I learned it meant *drunk* in Gaelic.

Toman looked back at me and whispered, "Watch, writer." Then he grabbed Sean from behind, a thick arm over his trachea muting his yelps. He dragged the Irishman back into a stall. A spastic fountain of urine shot from him, but the only sounds were his kicking heels dragging across the tiles, then the crack of bone inside the stall.

It was very fast, and by the time Toman had placed Sean on the toilet, shut the door, and started using paper towels to wipe the wet spots on his pants, I was still unsure what had just happened.

My body figured it out before my head did, and I threw myself into the next stall and regurgitated my ten pints.

"You was watching?" I heard him say behind me. "You watch, writer?"

I don't know exactly how, but soon we were out in the biting cold, Toman helping me walk and explaining that Sean's clients were from Belfast, laundering IRA proceeds by buying up most of Prague's old town.

"We kick out Russians, no? And now these Irish criminals, they think Toman will not to kick out them?"

We were in front of Sean's apartment, me trying to twist out of the Czech's grip. "You're a fucking murderer."

"And you are writer!" He helped me up the front steps as he jangled the keys he'd taken from Sean's body. "Toman help you find story. No?"

We were inside by this time, but I was still so goddamned cold.

"This is world, Writer. And now you see it. No more like you live in university."

It seems strange to me now, but I wasn't afraid of Toman. I was only repulsed and angry that he had pulled me into his putrid underworld.

"Fuck you, Toman."

"Fuck me?" he said, mimicking *Taxi Driver* with a big grin. "You do not see. Toman, he help his writer friend."

I dropped into a chair and didn't look at him. I spoke slowly so he'd understand. "All I see is that Toman is a psychopath who thinks killing someone is a good fucking *ha ha* to show his friends."

"But Toman—"

"I hate you."

He opened his mouth, then thought better of it. He started to button up his coat again. His voice was as wobbly as a dying man's stream of piss. "Toman, he work hard for his friends."

Then he left.

Over Sean's Becherovka, I considered going to the police— the Gardaí. That seemed reasonable. But after that, could I return to Prague? Toman didn't do this for just a *ha ha*—he was working for his Czechs, who wouldn't take kindly to my intervention.

Hell, I didn't even want to return to Bohemia now, and I didn't want to stay in Dublin. I knew what I'd do: I wouldn't talk to anyone. I'd just count my stuff in Prague—some clothes, a laptop with a terrible, pompous novel on it, and the paperback of that unreadable *Ulysses*—as losses and just fly home to Texas.

Then there was a knock on the door.

"Yes?"

"Garda. Open up."

I was faced with a big man. He wasn't dressed like a cop, but he had a badge. "Garda Jack Taylor," he told me, just in case I couldn't read. "Your name?"

I told him.

"Yank?"

I nodded.

"And what might you be doing in Sean MacDougal's flat?"

I started to answer something not far from a lie, then stepped back. Life's full of decisions that you end up going back on. "Want to come in?"

I told him the story straight through, but he was only half-listening, preoccupied with scanning the room for evidence of some kind. He walked around to a cabinet and brought a shot glass back with him. When I finished, he said, "So you're a writer, eh?"

I nodded.

"Good on you." He poured some Becherovka into the glass, said, "*Sláinte,*" and threw it back. "Don't get much better than McBain."

I admitted I'd never read the man, but quickly added that I was a Joyce fan.

That didn't impress him—no one in Dublin gave a damn about their most famous son. He pulled out a pack of reds and popped one in his mouth, eyeing me as if my reading preference had proven I was a faggot. "Mister Steinhauer, I'll be straight with you. What we've got are three witnesses placing you at Bellamy's with the deceased. They saw you follow him into the toilet. They saw you leave quickly."

"Yes, I told you this."

"But there's no mention of a big Hungarian."

"Czech."

"Yeah, right."

He poured a second shot as I registered what he'd said. "That's impossible—Toman's over six feet!"

Taylor threw back the Becherovka and licked his teeth. "Maybe, Mister Steinhauer, you imagined him."

I'd once written a bad story about a man whose friend commits rape, then later learns there was no friend, and he was the rapist. It was a common literary conceit, but in real life? "Give me a break. He bought my plane ticket. He introduced me to Sean MacDougal. Sean wouldn't've let me stay here otherwise."

Taylor took the bottle again. "Dead men needn't invite you in."

This cop seemed content just to sit here and drink Sean's Becherovka, and I was developing a migraine trying to get my head around this. "Let me see that badge again."

Unconcerned, he handed it over. It was real, all right—as far as I could tell—but then I noticed something. "You don't work here. You're with the Galway force."

"I'm helping out the boys in Dublin." Taylor pursed his lips. "I'm a fucking saint."

I took the bottle from him and refilled my own glass. "Then where's your partner?"

"Eh?"

"Police don't visit a suspect alone. Not even in fucking Dublin."

Taylor looked at me a moment, with a grin that reminded me of Toman. He reached out for the bottle. I handed it to him. "Aye, Mister Steinhauer, one thing you should be quite clear on is this Sean MacDougal was a shite of the highest order. No one in Dublin or even the Republic of Ireland will mourn this bastard's leave-taking."

I boarded the 2 p.m. to Prague bleary-eyed. After Garda Jack Taylor left I'd continued with the Becherovka, but instead of putting me to sleep it only made me sick. And my 5 a.m. shower only made me feel dirtier.

Toman hadn't returned to the flat, and I didn't see him in the departures lounge. I didn't know what that meant. But after most everyone had settled into their seats, he appeared at the front of the plane, red-faced, as if he'd been running. He smiled hugely as he settled next to me.

"Almost, I was late."

I looked out the window. He smelled bad.

"I stay at friend's last night."

"Did your friend survive the night?"

"Ha! A writer's sense for the humor."

"Your other friend sends his best wishes," I told him. "He says thank you."

"What friend is this?"

I finally looked at him; his red cheeks glimmered with sweat. "That Garda, Jack Taylor."

"What I tell you?" he said, then patted my knee. "Toman, he is friend for whole world."

"You stink, Toman."

He sniffed, then wrinkled his nose. "I must to clean off this piss."

# WISH
## BY JOHN RICKARDS

F our days since I called in sick. I think.
I've been awake for three of them straight. I think.
My fellow Gardaí would piss themselves if they could
see me, no doubt. Then they'd have me committed.

But they don't know. They haven't seen. They're all out
getting drunk, or off fucking their wives, or fucking their mis-
tresses and lying about it to their wives, or passed out in front
of their TVs in their nice safe homes while I'm

fucking

dead.

And I don't know if even I believe it.

It started with Michael. A mental case, low-grade nut. We
have quite a few. A handful of pedophiles, stalkers, minor
assaults. Care in the community jobs, not criminal enough
to be locked up for good, criminal enough to be in and out
of the cells on a regular basis. Since jail seems to do fuckall by way of curing them—worse, many come out of it
even more damaged than they went in—my own policy is
not to arrest. Talk, threaten, watch, but don't arrest if possible. Jail only makes them more of a risk to everyone in the
long run.

Some of these guys are homeless, but not Michael. It's a
shithole of a flat, though, overlooking the railway tracks not
far from where they cross the Tolka, north of Dublin's city

center. Building that smells of boiled vegetables and cat piss. Walls the color of boiled vegetables and cat piss.

"That woman hasn't been poisoning your kitten, Michael. She doesn't even know who you are. She wouldn't know how to poison a kitten even if she wanted to."

"Could swear I've seen her—"

"No, you haven't. She hasn't done a thing. Trust me on this, okay? Jesus, they train me for this sort of thing, and believe me, if she was guilty I'd know and I'd have dealt with her. You've got to stop yelling at the woman and threatening her, Michael."

Sullen look. A child being unfairly chided. A flash of malice. I wish I could make him shut up. I wish I had some way to frighten him into behaving. Then, suddenly, there it is.

So I do it. I drop the threat. Let the genie out of the bottle.

"And you listen good to me, Michael. You leave that woman alone from now on, or else I'll send your name, address, and photo to Iron Kurt's Gay Nazi website."

Let me explain. I have a friend, Curt, who's funny, erudite, can hold his drink remarkably well, and happens to be gay. One night in Fallon's, the conversation turns to gay rights and marriage, a subject which he understandably feels strongly about. He speaks his piece, and someone else makes some comment about him being a "facist homo" or something. Funny in its stupidity. And so the remark resurfaces and transforms, blossoming into something so much more.

It helps that there's been trouble with a couple of neo-Nazi crackpots in the city on TV recently, even with the NSRUS pulling out of Ireland. Nazis make the best bad guys. Ask Indiana Jones. And I see a twitch of fear or homophobia in Michael's eyes.

"I'll do it," I tell him. "And you know what'll happen then . . ."

Of course, his mind fills in the blank with its own worst fears. He promises to be good.

And over the next few weeks, he is. And I trot out the same threat to other lunatics I have to deal with. And they don't see me as a punisher. Iron Kurt is the punisher. I'm just the messenger. So they don't even resent me for it.

My fellow Gardaí find the whole thing fucking funny. Some of them start using Kurt themselves. And Dublin sleeps safer at night. Kurt's out there, watching over them. A specter in the fog blowing in off the harbor, creeping upriver. A paper tiger keeping evil at bay.

One afternoon, I see William, one of our deranged, sitting in the doorway of a boarded-up shop with an Iron Cross badge pinned proudly to his battered old blue Leinster rugby top. Next to him is a scratched metal strongbox.

"Hey, William."

"It's . . . you're gonna beat me."

"Leave it alone, William. What's in the box?"

"They're mine, see."

"Fine. But show me what you've got."

"It's private. Mine."

"Last time we had this conversation, you had a petrol bomb on you. I just want to make sure you don't have another one. Anything else, you can keep."

He thinks, pops open the box. Inside, an untidy pile of black fur.

"Why are you carrying a bunch of dead rats around?" I ask.

"They pay me. It's my deal. Not yours."

"I've got no ambitions of being a rat-catcher. Who pays?"

JOHN RICKARDS // 139

"The big red building down Castleforbes Road. Food warehouse. To set traps. Ten cents a rat."

"And you get them from somewhere else, and they pay for them."

"Yeah. It's a good job."

"Good for you. What's with the Iron Cross?" I point at his chest.

"It's protection, is what. Keith saw Iron Kurt."

I try not to smile. "Yeah?"

"And he said, you wear stuff like this and you'll be okay."

"Unless you've been posted on his website."

"Well, yeah."

"While we're on the subject, you're keeping away from that playground, right?"

He nods vigorously. "Yeah. Never meant to do anything."

"Did Keith say what Iron Kurt looked like?"

"Yeah. A big guy, tall, built like a brick shithouse. Bald. With a beard. Tattoos all over."

The real Curt is 5'5" and built for comfort, not speed. Again, I stifle a smile. "Yeah, that sounds right. You'd better stay out of trouble, huh?"

Not long after, I see Keith himself. The shopping trolley that holds his worldly possessions has a bunch of plastic German soldiers on string looped all the way around it like fairy lights. Now that I'm looking for it, I start to notice similar items on most of the other nutcases in my patch.

A belt buckle like an Iron Cross around the neck. A pencil-drawn swastika. An SS-style shoulder patch. In one house in Clontarf, a guy named Terry has a toy soldier shrine in a foil-lined cardboard box.

Votive offerings. Symbols of fear, not worship, not support. Warding off Kurt and his unholy wrath.

I shouldn't be surprised. They all gather together in Duff Alley off East Wall Road to drink Tenants Super until someone passes out or pisses themselves. And they talk, and share stories. Chinese whispers. Some believe them, some don't. But they all listen.

They say Kurt's the son of an SS officer. They say he's raped and killed more than two hundred men. They say his website has more than a thousand followers, all over the world, who take perverse delight in making each victim last as long as possible. They say—and when I tell Curt this he practically wets himself laughing—that he has a fourteen-inch dick and that most of his victims die from blood poisoning caused by massive anal tearing.

Iron Kurt.

My creation. My Frankenstein. My cartoon monster.

And then Keith disappears. One day, gone. No one knows where. No one's seen him. They find his trolley round the corner from a soup kitchen on North Quay, but he never comes back for it. Shit happens, these people move on.

William stops picking up pay for his rats and vanishes from the hostel he's been staying at. Someone tells me he'd been beaten up and his badge taken a couple of days before.

I stop seeing Terry. When I go to his house, his toy soldier shrine is still there, but he's gone. The neighbor says the last they saw of him, he was going to get a pint of milk. A couple of the others disappear too.

Duff Alley gets very empty, and the conversation there becomes very muted. They get drunk, huddle together, and after dark they whisper that Iron Kurt has come for them. And now I'm

shit

scared.

Another trip to the piss-stained steps outside Michael's flat. He's almost the only one left, and I need to know what he knows. To find out if he can reassure me. Keith left for Cork. William found a winning lottery ticket in the street and moved to the Caribbean. Some other Gardaí told the Duff Alley crazies to get out, so they're meeting somewhere else now.

When I knock on the door, I hear a wet thudding noise from inside. When I try the handle, it's unlocked. When I should turn and run away, I push it open and walk in.

The sickly sweet smell of blood on the air. The acrid spike of human waste. The cloying taste of someone else's sweat. Michael lies in a crimson-splashed, naked tangle in the middle of his living room floor. The carpet around him soaked black with blood. Legs splayed at an unnatural angle, and pink-yellow ribbons of intestines running from the split and tattered gash that yawns between them.

He twitches, and I realize he's still alive.

"Michael? Can you hear me?"

Whimper. Twitch. One eye creaks open and fixes me with a stare of utter agony and shock.

"Who did this? What the fuck's going on?"

"It . . . Kurt . . . didn't . . ."

"Kurt? You're sure? Christ."

"Said . . . name . . . site . . . to punish . . . I didn't . . ."

I should be calling an ambulance. I should be calling my colleagues. "Where is he now?"

Michael's eye looks down. Pleading. Betrayed. *"You said . . . wouldn't . . . website . . . I . . . good . . ."*

He thinks I did it. "I didn't tell him," I say. "Jesus, Michael, I wouldn't even know how. I swear to you."

*"He . . . told . . ."* Michael smacks his lips. Dry mouth. Lost too much fluid already. Bleeding out. Dying.

"What did he tell you?"

*"No . . . he asked . . . who . . . gave my name . . ."* Smack. Smack. *"I . . . told him . . . you . . ."*

As Michael's head drops to the carpet, something thumps out in the stairwell and my heart jumps into my mouth. Again I think about running, but I don't. Again I think about calling the station, but to tell them what? That some kind of phantom is stalking lunatics on my beat?

I step outside, check the stairs with shaky steps and trembling hands. And there's nothing there.

When I come back down to Michael's flat, the body is gone. So is the blood that soaked the carpet a moment ago. Is the smell gone as well? I can't tell. But there's no sign that Michael was ever here. And was he—could I be imagining it? Could all this be in my head, a product of my own fear?

Fuck. Fuck.

When I search the flat, I can't see any of the protective trinkets the others had. He was an unbeliever.

I'm not. Not now.

When I walk away from Michael's, I see the tall figure of a bald man watching me from the trees on the far side of the park across the street. He's massive, and bare-chested. The dark outlines of tattoos that litter his skin flicker and swirl like flames. He points at me, long and hard, then slides back into the undergrowth.

* * *

So now it's been four days since then, since I called in sick. Since I barricaded myself into my flat, to wait for the end. In the yellow glare of the forty-watt bulb, in the air that reeks of stale sweat and fear, I'm protected by a butcher's knife and an Iron Cross. A spray-paint swastika on every wall. A replica of one of those Nazi imperial eagles they'd carry everywhere in those films. Terry's foil-lined box with his tableau of half a dozen toy German WWII soldiers.

Maybe they'll help me. I certainly won't step beyond their protective radius.

Because Kurt is coming to kill me. His creator. To close the circle. I'm the last one he's looking for here. And he won't let me go. I know it.

Soon I'll hear his footsteps on the stairs. Slow, heavy, deliberate.

*Thump.*

*Thump.*

*Thump.*

Be careful what you wish for, you just might get it.

# THE DEATH OF JEFFERS

BY KEVIN WIGNALL

H eg the Peg was the end of it. Marty had known from the start which creek he was up; this was just the confirmation on the whereabouts of the paddle. If it had won, he'd have been in the clear, or as near as made any difference.

True to its name, though, the first race had finished five minutes ago and Heg the Peg was still running. So much for Bob and his cast-iron tips, straight from the stable, the whole crowd of them laying money on it like it was the only horse in the race. If there was any cast-iron, it was in Heg the Peg's saddle.

So now Marty had two choices. First was finding some other way of raising two thousand euros by the end of the month—and frankly, that was looking about as likely as the stewards disqualifying every other horse in the last race. Second was borrowing the money off Hennessey and paying back the interest for the rest of his life.

Three choices—he could tell McKeon to sing for the money, leave Dublin, leave Ireland, and find a monastery in Bhutan that was recruiting. Four choices—his next fare could be some crazy American on his first trip to Dublin, wanting to hire him for the whole week, money no object. You never knew with the airport.

The door opened and Marty turned off the radio.

"Wynn's Hotel, please." English, in a suit, overnight bag;

no big tip here. The fare leaned over and handed him a piece of paper with an address on it. "Could you stop here on the way? I'll give you a good tip."

Marty glanced at the address. It wasn't far out of the way.

"No problem. First time in Dublin?"

"Yes it is."

Marty pulled away. He could probably take the guy around the houses and he wouldn't be any the wiser. He found himself going the direct route, though; that was why he ended up in positions like this in the first place—he was too honest for his own good.

He looked in the rearview. The fare looked like a civil servant, or someone who worked in life insurance, nondescript, late thirties, the kind of guy who was born to make up the numbers and get lost in the crowd. But he'd still offer him the same old patter.

"I suppose you'll be wanting to sample some of the good stuff while you're here?"

"Sorry?"

"Guinness."

"Oh." The fare smiled like it was something he wasn't used to. "Actually, I don't drink. Very rarely, anyway."

Marty nodded and said, "So what brings you here then?"

"Business." He smiled again, though he wasn't getting any better at it. "But I've been wanting to come to Ireland for a long time. I'm of Irish stock."

Jesus, who wasn't? The day he picked up a fare at that airport who *didn't* claim to have Irish blood, that was the day he'd win the lottery. Still, he put on his best "that's amazing" smile and said, "Really? What's your name?"

"Jeffers. Patrick Jeffers."

Well sure, anyone could call their kid Patrick, but he

wasn't so sure about the Jeffers bit. Didn't sound particularly Irish to him.

"Don't know any Jeffers. Must be a name from out west."

"I think it is." End of conversation.

Jeffers kept him waiting no more than two minutes. He went into the house empty-handed and came out with a briefcase. Now *that* was suspicious, no other way of looking at it, particularly some guy who'd never been to Dublin.

By the time he got him to the Wynn's, though, there was no doubt it was his first time here—he'd been looking out of the window like a tourist for the last ten minutes.

"That'll be twenty-two euros."

"Keep the change," said Jeffers, handing him thirty.

"That's kind of you, Mr. Jeffers. Enjoy your stay in Dublin."

One thousand nine hundred and ninety-two to go.

Bryan was a charmer, all right, and there was no doubt about what he thought he'd be getting when they went out later. First day on the job, all the girls had told Kate not to fall for any of his talk, and here she was, second day behind the reception desk, going out with him tonight.

She was smiling at him now as he leaned across the desk. And he thought she was smiling at the silver words coming from his mouth, but it was how much he looked like Danny that was really tickling her. If it weren't for Bryan's blue eyes, the two of them could meet and think they were long-lost brothers.

Of course, Bryan would be the good brother. They all thought she was some naïve young slip of a thing, but twenty-four hours had been enough to tell her that Bryan was decent to the core. He was one for the girls, sure, but a good family lad at heart, working his way through college, a bright future ahead of him.

Danny, on the other hand, he was sexy and dangerous and the biggest mistake she'd made in her eighteen years. He'd come to a nasty end sooner or later and probably take a good few with him. The important thing was knowing that Danny wouldn't stick around, and that she wouldn't want him to.

Suddenly, Bryan pushed himself up and stepped away, making himself busy, and she saw one of the guests heading toward the desk, a businessman, boring-looking. She put on her best smile.

"Yes sir, what can I do for you?"

"I checked in a short while ago?"

He sounded like he was asking a question, and she felt like telling him straight, *Mister, if you don't remember, I sure as hell don't.* He certainly didn't look familiar.

"That's right. Is your room satisfactory, Mr. . . . ?"

"Jeffers."

"Mr. Jeffries, that's it."

"It's fine. But it's Mr. *Jeffers.* Actually, it's an Irish name."

"It is so. From up north, I think, Donegal, that way."

"Yes, I think you're right." He smiled, wonky somehow, like he'd had botox and was still getting used to his face again. "How do I get to Trinity College?"

"Ah, you have to work really hard at school." His smile stayed fixed—no sense of humor. "Just a little joke there. It's right around the corner. Bryan here will point the way."

Bryan had been straightening leaflets but snapped to attention now and ushered the Englishman out onto the street. He was cute, Bryan, a tight little backside on him, and he was going to get exactly what he wanted tonight, and the dates would be close enough that he'd never think to question whether the kid was his. How could he? In all probability, it was even going to look like him.

Jeffers had listened attentively as Bryan gave him directions for the short walk across to Trinity, but he seemed in no mood to move anywhere once he'd finished. So Bryan stood in silence with him, the two of them surveying the street like they were looking out over their ranch at sunset.

Then, absentmindedly, Jeffers said, "Have *you* heard of the name? Jeffers?"

"I haven't. Sorry." Jeffers nodded but still looked straight ahead, feet planted firmly, so Bryan tried to fill the pause by saying, "I'm a student at Trinity myself. History."

Jeffers turned and looked at him as if he'd revealed something vital. He stared at him for a few seconds, a look intense enough to be unnerving, and Bryan couldn't help but see that Jeffers seemed troubled. Finally, he said, "Let me tell you something: Don't ever fall into the trap of believing you don't have choices. You always have a choice, in everything."

He seemed to consider that for a moment, then nodded to himself and handed Bryan five euros before walking off along the street with Bryan's thanks lost in the noise behind him. Bryan stood there looking at the five euros, wondering what might have induced such a bizarre fit of profundity.

He was close to laughing it off as he walked back into the hotel, ready to get another smile out of Kate by telling her, and then for some reason it made him think of Lucy and it was no longer funny. *You always have a choice, in everything.* Lucy—if ever a girl could have turned him into a poet.

It was strange, though—two minutes with an English businessman who didn't know how to smile, and suddenly he felt that if he didn't get in touch with Lucy right now, see her this very evening, he'd regret it for the rest of his life. What was that all about?

Kate was smiling at him as he walked toward the desk. She was a pretty girl, and Danny had said she was easy, but he wasn't sure he wanted it anymore, not with her, not with any of these other girls.

"I've just got to make a call." She smiled back at him, coquettishly, he thought, but girl, it wouldn't be tonight.

"Mr. Parker, you do not have to write essays on Joyce, and when we're discussing him, I will not mark you down for opting out of the conversation, but if you insist on writing essays and speaking your mind, please be so kind as to read something other than *Dubliners.*"

The others laughed but Parker was smiling, too. She only teased him because she knew he could take it and because he was probably smarter than all the rest put together.

"You know, Dr. Burns, I have skim-read *Ulysses.*"

"Would that be the jogging tour of Dublin, Mr. Parker?" That earned another laugh, but the hour was upon them and they were already putting their things together. Parker was first out the door. Clare was the last, waiting till everyone had left before shyly handing in an essay.

She started to read through it once she was on her own again, but was only a page or two in—impressive, if lacking a little in flair—when there was a knock at the door and it opened a fraction.

"Come in."

The man who stepped into the room was about thirty-five, six foot, the average kind of build that couldn't easily be read under a suit. Facially, he looked innocuous, which immediately put her on guard.

"Dr. Elizabeth Burns?" She nodded, smiling, and he closed the door behind him.

"Call me Liz, Mr. . . . ?"

She'd gestured at the seat across from her desk, and as he sat down and placed his briefcase in front of him, he said, "Patrick Jeffers. The office sent me."

*The office.* It was about twenty years since she'd heard anyone call it that.

"And what office would that be?"

He didn't answer, just smiled awkwardly and relaxed into his seat.

He seemed to relax then, confident and in control as he said, "I've got a lot of admiration for people like you." She offered him a quizzical expression. No one had ever contacted her like this, so whoever he was, she wanted to draw him out a little more. "People in 14. And no, I don't expect you to admit it, but being buried deep the way you were for, what was it, four years, that really takes something."

Her expression unnerved him a little, and with no wonder, for she was wearing a look of utter astonishment. "Mr. Jeffers, I have absolutely no idea what you're talking about. People in 14 *what?*"

He nodded knowingly, uncomfortable, as if he'd spoken out of turn and made himself look unprofessional, which he had. At the same time, she was unnerved herself, wondering what this Jeffers was doing here, wondering why she'd had no word that he was coming. He knew she'd been in 14, so somebody must have sent him.

"You don't sound Irish." He tilted his head questioningly. "Jeffers is an Irish name, but you don't sound Irish. Irish grandparents, perhaps?"

"Yes, I think so." He hesitated before saying, "So you've

heard of the name? I think you're the first person since I arrived who recognizes it."

"There's actually a folk song, somewhere down in the southwest, though the exact location escapes me at the moment, about the death of a Jeffers."

"Oh, I didn't know that."

"Of course, there's also the American poet, Robinson Jeffers."

"Yes."

She could tell he didn't like being sidetracked. He was here on business and wanted to get on with it. "What do you want here, Mr. Jeffers? Why has your office sent you?"

"Yes, I'm really just here to deliver a message." He bent down and picked up his briefcase, but started to cover himself, saying, "Just some paperwork you need to read and sign."

*Amateur!* He was opening the briefcase on his lap and she had absolutely no doubt what kind of message he was about to produce from it. There were all kinds of thoughts running through her head, questions of whether she'd been double-crossed, and if so, by whom, questions of who he was working for and whether she'd have to move on, but there was something more immediate, an instinctive reflex that would never leave her.

She picked the phone up off the desk and threw it hard. It cracked him on the head with a clatter, and then a further clatter as the briefcase and the gun inside it fell onto the floor. He was dazed for only a second, but she was around the desk before he came up for air and she was pulling the telephone cord tight around his neck.

"Who sent you?"

His arms flailed, trying to strike her a body blow but unable to find her where she stood directly behind him.

"Who sent you?"

He took another approach, trying to pull her hands off, then trying to get his fingers under the cord, desperately tearing at his neck, drawing blood with his fingernails. He wouldn't talk; he was at least that professional. She yanked up the tension an extra notch, and the flailing of the arms gave way to a more convulsive movement through his entire body. She had to use all her strength to keep him in the seat, but she couldn't resist leaning down, whispering breathlessly into his ear.

"You know that song about Jeffers? It's a celebration. See, Jeffers was a diamond trader, and he was English."

She couldn't get the phone working again, even after she'd disentangled it from his body. She took her cell phone and dialed. When Lambert picked up, she said, "Someone came after me. I'll need removals."

"Someone from the north?"

"No, he claimed to be one of us."

"Name?"

"Patrick Jeffers. Passport backs that up." She looked at the passport she'd retrieved from his jacket. He certainly had the right look.

"Jeffers? There has to be a mistake. Let me just check something." She could hear Lambert tapping away on his computer keyboard. He was as much an old-timer as she was and always hit the keys like they belonged on a manual type-writer. "Liz, Patrick Jeffers is on his first assignment, but he's in Damascus; he's a Middle East specialist."

She looked at the throttled body, slumped in the chair like a drunk, and now that she thought of it, he hadn't seemed to recognize the name of Robinson Jeffers, and surely he would have, as surely as she knew who Robbie Burns was.

"Well, I hope he's doing better than the Jeffers in front of me now."

Lambert laughed. She liked Lambert; he had a good sense of humor. People didn't need to look much in this game, but a sense of humor was an absolute must.

# PART IV

NEW WORLD NOIR

# THE HONOR BAR

BY LAURA LIPPMAN

He took all his girlfriends to Ireland, as it turned out. "All" being defined as the four he had dated since Moira, the inevitably named Moira, with the dark hair and the blue eyes put in with a dirty finger. (This is how he insisted on describing her. *She* would never have used such a hackneyed phrase in general and certainly not for Moira, whose photographic likeness, of which Barry happened to have many, showed a dark-haired, pale-eyed girl with hunched shoulders and a pinched expression.)

When he spoke of Moira, his voice took on a lilting quality, which he clearly thought was Irish, but sounded to her like the kind of singsong voice used on television shows for very young children. She had dark HAIR and pale BLUE eyes put in with a DIRTY FINGER. Really, it was like listening to one of the Teletubbies wax nostalgic, if one could imagine Po (or La-La or Winky-Dink, or whatever the faggotty purple one was named) hunched over a pint of Guinness in a suitably picturesque Galway bar. It was in such a bar that Barry, without making eye contact, explained how he had conceived this trip to exorcise the ghost of Moira, only to find that it had brought her back in full force (again), and he was oh so sorry, but it was just not to be between them and he could not continue this charade for another day.

So, yes, the above—the triteness of his speech, its grating quality, his resemblance to a Guinness-besotted Teletubby—

was what she told herself afterward, the forming scab over the hurt and humiliation of being dumped two weeks into a three-week tour of the Emerald Isle. (And, yes, guess who called it that.) After her first, instinctive outburst—"You asshole!"—she settled down and listened generously, without recriminations. It had not been love between them. He was rich and she was pretty, and she had assumed it would play out as all her relationships did, for most of them had been based on that age-old system of give-and-take, quid pro quo, parting gifts. Twelve to twenty months, two to three trips, several significant pieces of jewelry. Barry was pulling the plug prematurely, that was all, and Ireland barely counted as a vacation in her opinion. It had rained almost every day and the shopping was shit.

Still, she nodded and interjected at the proper moments, signaling the pretty waitress for another, then another, all for him. She nursed her half-pint well into the evening. At closing time, she slipped the waitress twenty euros, straight from Barry's wallet, and the young woman obligingly helped to carry-drag Barry through the streets to the Great Southern. His eyes gleamed a bit as she and the waitress heaved him on the bed, not that he was anywhere near in shape for the award he was imagining.

(And just how did his mind work, she wondered in passing, how did a man who had just dumped a woman two weeks into a three-week trip persuade himself that the dumpee would then decide to honor him with a going-away threesome? True, she had been a bit wild when they first met. That was how a girl got a man like Barry, with a few decadent acts that suggested endless possibilities. But once you had landed the man, you kept putting such things off, suggested that the blowjob in the cab would follow the trip to Tiffany's, not vice versa, and pretty soon he was reduced to begging for the most ordinary favors.)

No, she and her new accomplice tucked Barry in properly and she tipped the waitress again, sending her into the night. Once the girl was gone, she searched his luggage and selected several T-shirts of which he was inordinately fond. These she ripped into strips, which she then used to bind his wrists and ankles to the four-poster bed. She debated with herself whether she needed to gag him—he might awaken, and start to struggle—and decided it was essential. She disconnected the phone, turned the television on so it would provide a nice steady hum in the background, then helped herself to his passport, American Express card, and all the cash he had. As Barry slept the rather noisy sleep of the dead-drunk, snorting and sawing and blubbering, she raided the minibar—wine, water, cashews. She was neither hungry nor thirsty, but the so-called honor bar was the one thing that Barry was cheap about. "It's the principle," he said, but his indignation had a secondhand feel to it, something passed down by a parent. Or, perhaps, a girlfriend. Moira, she suspected. Moira had a cheap look about her. She opened a chocolate bar, but rejected it. The chocolate here didn't taste right.

They were e-ticketed to Dublin, but that was a simple matter. She used the room connection to go online—cost be damned—and rearranged both their travel plans. Barry was now booked home via Shannon, while she continued on to Dublin, where she had switched hotels, choosing the Merrion because it sounded expensive and she wanted Barry to pay. And pay and pay and pay. Call it severance. She wouldn't have taken up with Barry if she hadn't thought he was good for at least two years.

It had been Barry's plan to send *her* home, to continue to

Dublin without her, where he would succumb to a mounting frenzy of Moira-mourning. That's what he had explained in the pub last night. And he still could, of course. But she thought there might be a kernel of shame somewhere inside the man, and once he dealt with the missing passport and the screwed-up airline reservations, he might have the good sense to continue home on the business-class ticket he had offered her. ("Yes, I brought you to Ireland only to break up with you, but I am sending you home business class.") He was not unfair, not through and through. His primary objective was to be rid of her, as painlessly and guiltlessly as possible, and she had now made that possible. He wouldn't call the police or press charges, or even think to put a stop on the credit card, which she was using only for the hotel and the flight back.

Really, she was very fair. Honorable, even.

"Mr. Gardner will be joining me later," she told the clerk at the Merrion, pushing the card toward him, and it was accepted without question.

"And did you want breakfast included, Mrs. Gardner?"

"Yes." She wanted everything included—breakfast and dinner and laundry and facials, if such a thing were available. She wanted to spend as much of Barry's money as possible. She congratulated herself for her cleverness, using the American Express card, which had no limit. She could spend as much as she liked at the hotel, now that the number was on file.

It was time, as it turned out, that was hard to spend. For all Barry's faults—a list that was now quite long in her mind, and growing every day—he was a serious and sincere traveler, the kind who made the most of every destination. He was a tourist in the best sense of the word, a man determined to wring experience from wherever he landed. While in Galway, they had rented a car and tried to follow Yeats's trail, figuratively and literally, driving south to see his castle and the swans at Coole, driving north to Mayo and his final resting place in the shadow of Ben Bulben, which Barry had confused with the man in the Coleridge poem. She had surprised Barry with her bits of knowledge about the poet, bits usually gleaned seconds earlier from the guidebook, which she skimmed covertly while pretending to look for places to eat lunch. Skimming was a great skill, much underrated, especially for a girl who was not expected to be anything but decorative.

It had turned out that Yeats's trail was also Moira's. Of course. Moira had been a literature major in college and she had a penchant for the Irish and a talent, apparently, for making clever literary allusions at the most unlikely moments. On Barry and Moira's infamous trip, which had included not just Ireland, but London and Edinburgh, Moira had treated Barry to a great, racketing bit of sex after seeing an experimental production of *Macbeth* at the festival. And while the production came off with mixed results, it somehow inspired a most memorable night with Moira, or so Barry had confided over all those pints in Galway. She had brought him to a great shuddering climax, left him spent and gasping for breath, then said without missing a beat: "Now go kill Duncan." (When the story failed to elicit whatever tribute Barry thought its due—laughter, amazement at Moira's ability to make Shakespearean allusions after sex—he had added, "I guess you had to be there." "No thank you," she had said.)

She did not envy Moira's education. Education was overrated. A college dropout, *she* had supported herself very well throughout her twenties, moving from man to man, taking on the kind of jobs that helped her meet the right kind of guys—galleries, catering services, film production offices. Now she was thirty—well, possibly thirty-one, she had been lying about her age for so long, first up, then down, that she got a little confused. She was thirty or thirty-one, possibly thirty-two, and while going to Dublin had seemed like an inspired bit of revenge against Barry, it was not the place to find her next patron, strong euro be damned. Paris, London, Zurich, Rome, even Berlin—those were the kind of places where a certain kind of woman could meet the kind of man who would take her on for a while. Who was she going to meet in Dublin? Bono? But he was married and always prattling about poverty.

So, alone in Dublin, she wasn't sure what to do, and when she contemplated what Barry might have done, she realized it was what Moira might have done, and she wanted no part of that. Still, somehow—the post office done, Kilmainham done, the museums done—she found herself in a most unimpressive town house, studying a chart that claimed to explain how parts of *Ulysses* related to the various organs of the human body.

"Silly, isn't it?" asked a voice behind her, startling her, not only because she had thought herself alone in the room, but also because the voice expressed her own thoughts so succinctly. It was an Irish voice, but it was a sincere voice, too, the beautiful vowels without all the bullshit blarney, which was growing tiresome. She could barely stand to hail a cab anymore because the drivers exhausted her so, with their outsized personalities and long stories and persistent questions. She couldn't bear to be alone, but she couldn't bear all the conversation, all the *yap-yap-yap-yap-yap* that seemed to go with being Irish.

"It's a bit much," she agreed.

"I don't think any writer, even Joyce, thinks things out so thoroughly before the fact. If you ask me, we just project all this symbolism and meaning onto books to make ourselves feel smarter."

"I feel smarter," she said with an automatic smile, "just talking to you." It was the kind of line in which she specialized, the kind of line that had catapulted her from one safe haven to the next, Tarzan swinging on a vine from tree to tree.

"Rory Malone," he added, offering his hand, offering the next vine. His hair was raven-black, his eyes pale-blue, his lashes thick and dark. Oh, it had been so long since she had been with anyone good-looking. It was something she had learned to sacrifice long ago. Perhaps Ireland was a magical place after all.

"Bliss," she said, steeling herself for the inane things that her given name inspired. "Bliss Dewitt." Even Barry, not exactly quick on the mark, had a joke at the ready when she provided her name. But Rory Malone simply shook her hand, saying nothing. A quiet man, she thought to herself, but not *The Quiet Man*. Thank God.

"How long are you here for?"

They had just had sex for the first time, a most satisfactory first time, which is to say it was prolonged, with Rory extremely attentive to her needs. It had been a long time since a man had seemed so keen on her pleasure. Oh, other men had tried, especially in the beginning, when she was a prize to be won, but their best-intentioned efforts usually fell a little short of the mark and she had grown so used to faking it that the real thing almost caught her off guard. Nice.

"How long are you staying here?" he persisted. "In Dublin, I mean."

"It's . . . open-ended." She could leave in a day, she could leave in a week. It all depended on when Barry cut off her credit. His credit, really. How much guilt did he feel? How much guilt should he feel? She was beginning to see that she might have gone a little over the edge where Barry was concerned. He had brought her to Ireland and discovered he didn't love her. Was that so bad? If it weren't for Barry, she never would have met Rory, and she was glad she had met Rory.

"Open-ended?" he said. "What do you do that you have such flexibility?"

"I don't really have to worry about work," she said.

"I don't worry about it, either," he said, rolling to the side and fishing a cigarette from the pocket of his jeans.

That was a good sign—a man who didn't have to worry about work, a man who was free to roam the city during the day. "Let's not trade histories," she said. "It's tiresome."

"Good enough. So what do we talk about?"

"Let's not talk so much either."

He put out his cigarette and started again. It was even better the second time, better still the third. She was sore by morning, good sore, that lovely burning feeling on the inside. It would probably lead to a not-so-lovely burning feeling in a week or two and she ordered some cranberry juice at breakfast that morning, hoping it could stave off the mild infection that a sex binge brought with it. *Honeymooners-cystitis*, as her doctor called it.

"So Mr. Gardner has finally joined you," the waiter said, used to seeing her alone at breakfast.

"Yes," she said.

"I'll have a soft-boiled egg," Rory said. "And some salmon. And some of the pancakes?"

"Slow down," Bliss said, laughing. "You don't have to try everything at one sitting."

"I have to keep my strength up," he said, "if I'm going to keep my lady happy."

She blushed and, in blushing, realized she could not remember the last time she had felt this way. It was possible that she had never felt this way.

"Show me the real Dublin," she said to Rory later that afternoon, feeling bold. They had just had sex for the sixth time and, if anything, he seemed to be even more intent on her needs.

"This is real," he said. "The hotel is real. I'm real. How much more Dublin do you need?"

"I'm worried there's something I'm missing."

"Don't worry. You're not."

"Something authentic, I mean. Something the tourists never see."

He rubbed his chin. "Like a pub?"

"That's a start."

So he took her to a pub, but she couldn't see how it was different from any other pub she had visited on her own. And Rory didn't seem to know anyone, although he tried to smoke and professed great surprise at the new anti-smoking laws. "I smoke here all the time," he bellowed in more or less mock outrage, and she laughed, but no one else did. From the pub, they went to a rather depressing restaurant—sullen wait-staff, uninspired food—and when the check arrived, he was a bit slow to pick it up.

"I don't have a credit card on me," he said at last—

sheepishly, winningly—and she let Barry pay. Luckily, they took American Express.

Back in bed, things were still fine. So they stayed there more and more, although the weather was perversely beautiful, so beautiful that the various hotel staffers who visited the room kept commenting on it.

"You've been cheated," said the room-service waiter. "Ask for your money back. It's supposed to rain every day, not pour down sunlight like this. It's unnatural, that's what it is."

"And is there no place you'd like to go, then?" the chambermaid asked when they refused her services for the third day running, maintaining they didn't need a change of sheets or towels.

Then the calls began, gentle but firm, running up the chain of command until they were all but ordered out of the room by the hotel's manager so the staff could have a chance to clean. They went, blinking in the bright light, sniffing suspiciously at the air, so fresh and complex after the recirculated air of their room, which was now a bit thick with smoke. After a few blocks, they went into a department store, where Rory fingered the sleeves of soccer jerseys. *Football*, she corrected herself. Football jerseys. She was in love with an Irishman. She needed to learn the jargon.

"Where do you live?" she asked Rory, but only because it seemed that someone should be saying something.

"I have a room."

"A bed-sit?" She had heard the phrase somewhere, perhaps from a London girl with whom she had worked at the film production office. Although, come to think of it, Ireland and England apparently were not the same, so the slang might not apply.

"What?"

"Never mind." She must have used it wrong.

"I like this one." He indicated a red-and-white top. She had the distinct impression that he expected her to buy it for him. Did he think she was rich? That was understandable, given the hotel room, her easy way with room service, not to mention the minibar over the past few days. They had practically emptied it. All on Barry, but Rory didn't know that.

Still, it seemed a bit cheesy to hint like this, although she had played a similar game with Barry in various stores and her only regret was that she hadn't taken him for more, especially when it came to jewelry. Trips and meals were ephemeral and only true high-fashion clothing—the classics, authentic couture—increased in value. She was thirty-one. (Or thirty, possibly thirty-two.) She had only a few years left in which to reap the benefits of her youth and her looks. Of course, she might marry well, but she was beginning to sense she might not, despite the proposals that had come her way here and there. Then again, it was when you didn't care that men wanted to marry you. What would happen as thirty-five closed in? Would she regret not accepting the proposals made, usually when she was in a world-class sulk? Marriage to a man like Barry had once seemed a life sentence. But what would she do instead? She really hadn't thought this out as much as she should.

"Let's go back to the room," she said abruptly. "They must have cleaned it by now."

They hadn't, not quite, so the two of them sat in the bar, drinking and waiting. It was early to drink, she realized, but only by American standards. In Rory's company, she had been drinking at every meal except breakfast and she wasn't sure she had been completely sober for days.

Back in the room, Rory headed for the television set,

clicking around with the remote control, then throwing it down in disgust. "I can't get any scores," he said.

"But they have a crawl—"

"Not the ones I want, I mean." He looked around the room, restless and bored, and seemed to settle on her only when he had rejected everything else—the minibar, the copy of that morning's *Irish Times*, a glossy magazine. Even then, his concentration seemed to fade midway through, and he patted her flank. She pretended not to understand, so he patted her again, less gently, and she rolled over. Rory was silent during sex, almost grimly so, but once her back was to him, he began to grunt and mutter in a wholly new way, and when he finished, he breathed a name into the nape of her neck.

Trouble was, it wasn't hers. She wasn't sure whose it was, but she recognized the distinct lack of her syllables—no "Bluh" to begin, no gentle hiss at the end.

"What?" she asked. It was one thing to be a stand-in for Barry when he was footing the bills, to play the ghost of Moira. But she would be damned before she would allow a freeloader such as Rory the same privilege.

"What?" he echoed, clearly having no idea what she meant.

"Whose name are you saying?"

"Why, Millie. Like in the novel, *Ulysses*. I was pretending you were Millie and I was Bloom."

"It's Molly, you idiot. Even I know that." Again, a product of a quick skim of the cards on the museum's wall. But *Millie*? How could he think it was Millie?

"Molly. That's what I said. A bit of play-acting. No harm in that."

"Bullshit. I'm not even convinced that it was a woman's name you were saying."

"Fuck you. I don't do guys."

His accent had changed—flattened, broadened. He now sounded as American as she did.

"Where are you from?"

He didn't answer.

"Do you live in Dublin?"

"Of course I do. You met me here, didn't you?"

"Where do you live? What do you do?"

"Why, here. And this." He tried to shove a hand beneath her, but she felt sore and unsettled, and she pushed him away.

"Look," he said, his voice edging into a whine. "I've made you happy, haven't I? Okay, so I'm not *Irish*-Irish. But my, like, ancestors were. And we've had fun, haven't we? I've treated you well. I've earned my keep."

Bliss glanced in the mirror opposite the bed. She thought she knew what men saw when they looked at her. She had to know; it was her business, more or less. She had always paid careful attention to every aspect of her appearance—her skin, her hair, her body, her clothes. It was her only capital and she had lived off the interest, careful never to deplete the principle. She exercised, ate right, avoided drugs, and, until recently, drank only sparingly—enough to be fun, but not enough to wreck her complexion. She was someone worth having, a woman who could captivate desirable men—economically desirable men, that is—while passing hot hors d'oeuvres, or answering a phone behind the desk at an art gallery.

But this was not the woman Rory had seen, she was realizing. Rory had not seen a woman at all. He had seen clothes. He had seen her shoes, high-heeled Christian Lacroix that were hell on the cobblestones. And her bag, a Marc Jacobs slung casually over the shoulder of a woman who could afford to be casual about an $1,800 bag because she had far more expensive ones back home. Only "home" was Barry's apartment, she realized, and lord knows what he had done with her things. Perhaps that was why he hadn't yet alerted the credit card company—he was back in New York, destroying all her possessions. He would be pissed about the T-shirts, she realized somewhat belatedly. They were vintage ones, not like the fakes everyone else was wearing now, purchased at Fred Segal's last January.

And then she had brought Rory back to this room, this place of unlimited room service and the sumptuous breakfasts and the "Have-whatever-you-like-from-the-minibar" proviso. She had even let him have the cashews.

"You think I'm rich," she said.

"I thought you looked like someone who could use some company," Rory said, stretching and then rising from the bed.

"How old are you?" she asked.

"Twenty-four."

He was she, she was Barry. How had this happened? She was much too young to be an older woman. And nowhere near rich enough.

"What do you do?"

"Like I said, I don't worry about work too much." He gave her his lovely grin, with his lovely white, very straight teeth. American teeth, like hers, she realized now.

"Was I . . . work?"

"Well, as my dad said, do what you love and you'll love what you do."

"But you'd prefer to do men, wouldn't you? Men for fun, women for money."

"I told you, I'm no cocksucker," he said, and landed a quick, stinging backhand on her cheek. The slap was professional, expert, the slap of a man who had ended more than one argument this way. Bliss, who had never been struck in her life—except on the ass, with a hairbrush, by an early boyfriend who found that exceptionally entertaining—rubbed her cheek, stunned. She was even more stunned to watch Rory proceed to the minibar and squat before it, inspecting its restocked shelves.

"Crap wine," he said. "And I am sick to hell of Guinness and Jameson."

The first crack of the minibar door against his head was too soft; all it did was make him bellow. But it was hard enough to disorient him, giving Bliss the only advantage she needed. She straddled his back and slammed the door repeatedly on his head and neck. Decapitation occurred to her as a vague if ambitious goal. She barely noticed his hands reaching back, scratching and flailing, attempting to dislodge her, but her legs were like steel, strong and flexible from years of pilates and yoga. She decided to settle for motionlessness and silence, slamming the door on Rory's head until he was finally, blessedly still.

But still was not good enough. She wrested a corkscrew from its resting place—fifteen euros—and went to work. Impossible. Just as she was about to despair, she glanced at a happy gleam beneath the bedspread, a steak knife that had fallen to the floor after one of their room-service feasts and somehow gone undetected. Ha, even the maids at the oh-so-snooty Merrion weren't so damn perfect.

She kept going, intent on finishing what she had started, even as the hotel was coming to life around her—the telephone ringing, footsteps pounding down the corridors. She should probably put on the robe, the lovely white fluffy robe. She was rather . . . speckled.

But the staff came through the door before she could get to her feet.

"How old are you, then?" the police officer—they called them *Gardaí* here—asked Bliss.

"How old do I look?"

He did not seem to find her question odd. "You look like the merest slip of a girl, but our investigation requires more specific data."

He was being so kind and solicitous, had been nothing but kind all along, although Bliss sensed that the fading mark on her cheek had not done much to reconcile the investigators to the scene they had discovered in the hotel room. They tried to be gallant, professing dismay that she had been hit and insulted. But their shock and horror had shown through their professional armor. They clearly thought this was a bit much for a woman who insisted she had been doing nothing more than defending herself.

"Really? You're not just saying that?"

"I'd be surprised if you could buy a drink legally in most places."

Satisfied, she gave her real age, although it took a moment of calculation to get it right. Was she thirty or thirty-one, possibly thirty-two? She had added two years back in the early days, when she was starting out, then started subtracting three as of late.

"I'm thirty-one."

"That's young."

"I thought so."

# TOURIST TRADE
## BY JAMES O. BORN

I t might have been a death spasm or a reflex, but the man's hand flew up and his long, clean fingernails raked across Reed's face. He hardly reacted. So he had a scar to match the others now. His father had done worse to him by the time he was ten. This might be a tad more serious, as he could feel the blood trickle into his right eye. Reed leaned away so he wouldn't feel the man's last, moist breath. The knife was still firmly buried in the man's solar plexus. The long K-bar survival knife with a half-serrated edge had cut through his skin and into his heart like, well, like a sharp knife slicing through skin and heart. No wonder the U.S. Marines issued these things. Fucking Americans, they did everything too big. A seven-inch blade on a knife! That was three inches too many. The man coughed like he had been smoking Camels most his life—they were in Dublin, so it might have been true, but Reed had picked this fella because he looked like a tourist. That had been the first goal: always a visitor.

In this case, Reed had seen the man come from a pub off Swift's Row and simply fell in behind him. He was careful never to be seen with a victim. The first thing that tipped him to the man's lack of roots in Dublin was that he had on a yellow shirt under a blue windbreaker. No Dub worth his balls would be caught in such an obnoxious outfit. These Dubliners loved their black. Black shirts, black jackets, God help him but he had noticed even the kids favored black on their way to school. Must've made the weather look brighter by comparison. Not like home in the west.

Looking into the man's pale-blue eyes he pulled out the big K-bar, feeling the rough edge catch on some gristle and maybe the last rib. It sounded like his old man sawing on the Christmas turkey when he was a kid. More blood, but similar.

He examined his right hand with the latex surgical glove. It was uniformly red from the fingers to the wrist. The handle of the knife had a string of flesh or tendon hanging from it. Reed watched the man slide down the wall into a sitting position, then slump into his final posture. He didn't check for a pulse. If this bloke could survive that hacking, he deserved to live. Didn't matter anyway. An attack like this, even if someone survived it, still accomplished his mission.

He wiped his forehead with his left hand and realized he needed to stop the bleeding with a rag. He glanced around the alley. There was nothing obvious. He had stumbled into the cleanest alley in Dublin. Easing out toward the street he found a wad of newspaper and wiped his forehead. He ripped a section off for a makeshift bandage. Holding it to his face, he started on his way.

He headed out onto the empty street. Most the streets were empty now-a-days. People didn't feel safe in Dublin after dark. He had seen to that. As he came to Wellington Quay near the Millennium Bridge, he casually flipped the knife over the small seawall and into the water. The glove was tied around the handle and the neat little package made hardly a splash as it sank to the bottom of the channel. This was getting expensive. A new knife every time and the fucking K-bar cost nearly thirty-five euros. So far, with housing and food he'd spent a fortune on this endeavor. All for a righteous cause. That's how he looked at it. That's how he had to look at it.

He crossed the road after a few streets, making sure no one had seen him. His old man had always taken the long way home, but he was usually ducking a bookie or one of the other carpenters he'd borrowed money from and didn't intend to pay back. The long walks with his old fella had taught Reed patience and given him some endurance that had lasted all these years even though he was almost forty.

An hour later, he was close to Lucan and his favorite pub in Dublin, the Ball Alley House. He had stumbled onto it the first night he arrived in town and had been coming every night the last twenty days. He made sure the barmaid, Maura, always saw him and he tipped her well so if he ever had to explain to the Gardaí, he'd have an alibi and a witness. Besides, you could do worse than flirt with a young one with all her meat in the right places. Not that he'd stray. All he thought of most nights was seeing his Rose and the twins again. He wished they could have come with him, but he'd have had a hard time explaining his nights on the street.

After a stop in the loo to clean up and make sure his wound wasn't worse than he thought, he strolled to the bar. The barmaid, Maura, smiled as she walked over to him roosting on his favorite stool. She had a pint in her hand already.

"Brilliant, love, thanks so much."

The young barmaid from the north side smiled, revealing a missing tooth. "It's nothing. You're a tad late this evening."

"On the phone with my bride."

Maura's smile dimmed slightly, then she noticed his face. "What in the name of God happened to you?"

He touched the twin scratches the dead man's fingernails

had made on his forehead. "Low branches over near the Uni were thicker than they looked."

She eyed him like a wife who had caught her man stepping out, then without a word headed past him to another customer.

He leaned onto the walnut bar and took a gulp of the pint. At home he rarely visited pubs. Even with the new job he found himself more at restaurants or, occasionally, at hotel bars. The atmosphere seemed to soothe him.

He nodded as two men plopped onto the stools next to him. Maura was in front of them before they had looked up.

The older man, maybe sixty, next to him just said, "Pint." Maura knew to draw a Guinness stout. The other man, a good ten years younger and wearing a light sweater, said, "Harp, my dear."

The older man turned to him and in a loud voice said, "Harp, Jaysus Christ, didn't know I was drinking with a girl." He roared with laughter and looked around for support. Finding little, he settled back with his stout.

Reed cut his eyes to the loud older man who had what sounded like a Limerick accent. Too bad these two were at this bar. They would've been perfect except that he knew to never shit where you eat. But the longer they sat there the more enticing it became. The older one told bad joke after bad joke and then commented on every subject from the weather to the euro.

"I tell you, it's a German plot. They want a consistent currency for the next time they take over the continent. Just more convenient that way."

He and his friend finally started chatting about something of interest. The younger one said, "Things are quieter in here since the damn butcher's been roaming the streets."

"Aye, that's the Gospel truth. You'd think the Gardaí would be swoopin' in here like the wrath o' God."

Maura walked by adding, "Does nothing for our business and I don't walk home alone anymore. Three dead in three weeks. It's a shame."

The old man said, "Everyone's hurting, love. Restaurants are closing. The cinemas have three people per show. Even the airport is empty as more and more people hear about our problems."

Reed kept his mouth shut, not correcting the lovely barmaid that it was four dead in the three weeks. She'd know by tomorrow morning at the latest. Tomorrow would be his last one. That way he'd have plenty of people scared, and by doing it two nights in a row he avoided patterns the police would pick up on.

Reed said to Maura, "You know if Blue Balls are playing tonight?"

"No, they're only at the International on Saturdays. But with the trouble they may not be playing at all."

"A shame." He left some bills on the bar for her and headed out the door, nodding to the few regulars. It was good to be seen.

He slept soundly after a shower and a few minutes cleaning his scratches. He wasn't used to sleeping late. Usually the twins would start their day early by jumping into bed with him until he woke, pretended to be a monster, and tickled them until everyone had to lay back and catch their breath. The whole time the flat would fill with the smell of sausages as Rose prepared breakfast. It was a grand existence, but he didn't mind just lying in a big bed as the sun climbed a little higher behind the clouds that seemed to constantly surround Dublin.

By 10:00 he was out of bed and checking his forehead for any sign of infection. Aside from being fresh, they didn't look much different than the set of scratches he had on his neck from the day his old man lost twenty-five quid on some horse at Gowran Park. He shrugged. It was almost over and he'd be the toast of the town when he got back.

Later that day, as the sun began to set—at least he thought it was setting because it was getting dark though he couldn't actually see the sun—Reed stepped out of his hotel room and down through the main lobby. He had the last of the knives he had bought in Limerick. A sharp Gerber four-forty steel, with a four-inch blade. With luck he would have to toss it in the Liffey by 10 o'clock. As he turned toward the river, he heard a voice.

"Hang on there."

Reed turned to find a Dublin cop with hard brown eyes staring down at him. His dark-blue uniform had the name *Reily* on the left breast. The cop was near his age and looked to be in good shape. That might cause problems if things didn't go well.

Reed turned and faced the cop, conscious of the bandage he'd stuck over his scratch.

The cop walked over to him, eyeing his forehead. "What happened there, boyo?"

"Tree branch."

"What were ya doin' in a tree at your age?"

Reed wasn't sure if the cop was having a go at him or serious. "Low branch. I was walking."

The copper nodded and said, "Where you off to this time of night?"

"Six? This time of night is right for a pop before dinner."

The cop nodded at the answer. "Where d'ya go?"

"Usually the Ball Alley House."

The cop took in the information and stepped back. Reed tensed like he might be hit or more cops would swoop in and grab him. He had the knife on him. He'd hate to use it on this cop. He wiggled his hip and felt the knife in its scabbard snug against his waistband. He checked out the copper's uniform, trying to detect any kind of protective vest under it. Too hard to tell. Reed decided he'd have to stab him in the neck quick and deep. The only problem was that it would bring a lot of heat. He'd be gone, but it was a danger regardless.

The cop said, "Bollocks."

Reed just stared at the beefy man.

"Bakurs on Thomas or the Cukoos Nest beat the arse off the Ball Alley House."

Reed relaxed slightly. "Ah, it will have to do. That's my place."

The cop said, "You got a funny accent. Where you from?"

"Galway."

"What brings ya to the Big Smoke?"

Reed considered his answer as he calmly placed his hand on his hip, an inch from the knife. This would have to be fast.

An old Honda zipped around the corner and swerved to miss a trash bin in the road, nearly causing it to run down the cop. To make matters worse, the driver beeped at him. The cop hopped onto the sidewalk, pushing Reed away from the street too.

With the cop next to him and distracted, Reed reached under his loose shirt, gripped the hard handle of the Gerber, and prepared for a fluid motion of slashing up, then planting that thing right in the cop's thick neck.

But the cop jumped back into the street yelling, "You fucking rice-grinding shite!" Without a glance back at Reed, he trotted down the street and hopped into his small, unmarked car. Within twenty seconds the vehicle was racing past Reed toward the speeding Honda.

An hour later, Reed was behind a young American couple slowly strolling toward one of the local hotels. The five-story building had a decent restaurant and bar in the lobby. Reed hoped they were staying at the hotel and were on their way back instead of stopping for a bite and pint. He stayed back a ways until they were to the door of the hotel, then closed the distance to see where they were headed. The man was maybe thirty and built like a model, too thin and too neat. The woman was younger, about twenty-three and fresh-looking like a lot of the Americans from California or Florida. She had long blond hair and looked like she'd had to grease herself to slide into the Levi's gripping her hips.

Reed came up the front steps and almost knocked into them in the lobby. They had stopped to look over the restaurant's posted menu. Reed peered at the man. He wouldn't be thinking about a toasted sandwich if he had a girl like that stuck on his arm. Typical Yank.

He eased past them like he was heading to the lifts, and then a miracle happened. They followed him. It couldn't have been more natural. As he stood by the buttons, he asked the man, "What floor?"

He had a funny accent, even just saying, "Four, please."

Reed nodded and mumbled, "Me too," as he hit the button. He glanced over at the couple. The girl smiled at him with a dazzling spray of white.

Reed paused so they could get off the elevator, then followed them down the narrow hallway. The cheap carpet made a *swoosh* sound as they all glided along. His right hand was up on his hip.

The couple slowed at a room five from the end of the hall

and the man fumbled with the plastic card key. Reed heard the door click and then saw a crack of light from the inside. He was on the man right as he entered the doorway, knife out and slashing deep across his throat before the girl even turned to see what the funny noise was. He shoved the shocked man into the bathroom to his left and advanced down on the girl as she turned. Before she could say a word, he had a hand across her beautifully sculpted face and the knife deep into her solar plexus. He wiggled his hand, slicing through veins and heart tissue as he watched the life seep right out of her blue eyes. He pulled the blade out and sliced into her left breast, amazed at the clear liquid that gushed out before the blood. Fucking implants. Unnatural.

He carefully placed her on the wide, unmade bed, even setting her head on the pillow. Then he turned and stepped toward the bathroom. The man was motionless on the ground and the blood still seeped from the massive wound on his neck. Reed had to step away from the door as the red ocean threatened to flow over the threshold. He leaned in and snatched a white towel from inside the door and wiped down his bloody knife, then his hands. He twisted the towel and laid it across the door frame so it would stop the blood from spilling into the room. He didn't want anyone to find these two for as long as possible.

He checked his shoes quickly, reset the knife in its scabbard, took the *Do not disturb* sign from the inside door handle, and then opened the door. After hanging the sign, he casually walked back to the lift, more than satisfied with his last job. Now this whole ugly business was over. His own job secured, no one the wiser. As he waited for the lift, he made a quick check of his hands and found a splash of blood on the back of his right one.

The lift bell sounded and the doors parted. He looked up into a wide, round face that seemed familiar.

"Jaysus fucking Christ. What might Galway's new tourism director be doing in Dublin?" He smiled showing crooked, browning teeth. The lift doors closed behind him as he came up to Reed. "This whole butcher business has pushed every fucking tourist in the country to Galway."

Reed returned the smile, no easy task. "Hello, Jason, what're you doin' here?"

"Just passing through. I'm settin' up a network for the university. But I thought you'd be up to your arse in work back home."

"I return tomorrow," Reed said.

Jason said, "You never answered my question. What're you doin' here?"

Reed let a little smile cross his lips. "I better show you." He let his right hand come to his hip and started to lift his shirt as he slapped the emergency stop button with his left. He'd show the man just how far a good tourism director might go for his job.

# HEN NIGHT

BY SARAH WEINMAN

It took three tries before I understood what Deborah was saying. The first time I must have completely misheard; the second, I simply refused to believe it.

"You're absolutely shitting me," I said after the third try.

"Of course not, Andrea. When do I ever?"

She had a point. We'd known each other all our lives and Deborah never, ever joked around about anything. Let alone about where she wanted to have her hen night.

"But Dublin?" I tried to keep the panic out of my voice.

"Don't worry, I'm paying for everyone."

I gritted my teeth. Even though we'd been best friends almost since birth, Deborah always had the knack for reminding me that she'd been raised on the right side of the Jewish ghetto in Golders Green, while I'd been stuck in Temple Fortune—or rather, I'd had the misfortune to grow up there.

"That's not it. But Dublin? During Bank Holiday weekend? Are you barking mad? It'll be swarmed with idiotic drunks looking for a shag."

"And how's that different from any London pub? Besides, I want something special. And you've always wanted to go to Dublin, I thought. At least, that's what you say practically every other week."

I often wondered why I was still friends with her. Family ties, perhaps; our mothers met in university and still rang each other every morning to discuss the latest community gossip and which of their friends' children were misguided enough to break their parents' hearts and marry outside of the faith. That's why Deborah's engagement to Sam had been such a coup; his family was well-respected, he was a financier with London's oldest and finest, and best of all, he was Jewish. The community didn't realize he was a complete and utter asshole and that he and Deborah only stayed together because she had good tits and he was well-hung, but I tried to keep those opinions to myself.

Most of the time, I remembered why we remained mates. Yes, she could be a bitch, but she was utterly loyal; once she'd decided you were one of her friends, that was that, and she'd do anything she possibly could for you. She was blunt, and often too harsh, but her advice cut to the quick and was nearly always right. She also had a freakishly good memory, especially about what her friends wanted and ought to do with themselves.

That's why she was dead right about Dublin. I'd done Celtic studies at University College (to go with a more suitable biology major) and had spent a joyous summer after graduation traveling through Ireland. But for some inexplicable reason, I'd spent most of my time in and around Limerick, missing the capital city completely. In the two years since, I'd been chained to the lab at King's so much I'd barely left the South Bank, let alone had time for a proper vacation. I was certainly due.

"You have me there," I admitted. "So who else is coming?"

"Adele, Laura, Hannah, and Carol have said yes, though now that I think about it, I'm not so sure I should have invited Hannah. She's been such a cow about Sam. Is she going to be any fun?"

I shrugged. Hannah was the only one of us with the guts to tell Deborah her—and our—true feelings about him. In a group, Sam was all sweetness and light, but any time he caught one of us alone, his hands started wandering and his speech turned filthy. The last time he'd tried something on me, I stamped my foot on his ankle until he finally screamed and left. That was six months ago.

"I'm sure Hannah is just trying to be helpful," I said. "And you'd feel awful if you didn't invite her."

"You're so right. This is so exciting! My last hurrah as a single woman and all my best friends will be with me. It'll be fantastic!"

I said no more.

A month later, the six of us boarded a Ryanair plane and spent the hour-long flight catching up. It was the first time in a year we'd all been together, and as the noise level increased, I remembered why I'd always begged off: There was something about women in groups that made my skin crawl. One-on-one was fine, but *en masse,* I remembered these were Deborah's friends, not mine; that she'd befriended each of them in primary school or uni or at work, and that I had little in common with them.

It was bad form to take out the crime novel I was only pages away from finishing, so I pretended to take part in the conversation. Thank God it was a short flight.

As I stared into space, I heard a snatch of conversation from behind me.

"Did you see Sam before you left?"

"No, Carol. He left a message saying he was stuck at work."

"Typical, isn't it?"

"I know, but he's a very busy man, what could he do?"

Hannah cut in. "Too busy to say goodbye to his fiancée? Ridiculous."

I tuned them out. I thought about what I would do when I finally reached Dublin. I had no desire to see the usual tourist crap, but didn't expect anyone else to share my interest in lesser-known haunts. No doubt they'd spend most of their time shopping.

Sure enough, once we'd arrived and settled ourselves in the hotel bar, Adele announced to loud approving noises that she wanted to go to Grafton Street "to see what Dublin deems high fashion."

I declined. "I'm rather knackered at the moment. What say we meet up back here at 8 o'clock before going to Temple Bar?"

"That'll do. Enjoy . . . whatever it is you'll be doing," said Deborah.

I lay down in my room for a few minutes but quickly grew restless. I had a pilgrimage to make. After asking the concierge for directions, a ten-euro cab ride took me outside the premises of the Irish-Jewish Museum in the Portobello district. The building was a lot smaller than I'd imagined, and the actual museum was even tinier: a room filled with mementos of several lost Irish-Jewish communities and an entire section devoted to Chaim Herzog, the Dublin-born former President of Israel.

The curator, a stout woman in her late thirties, looked almost apologetic. "The communities were very small, and they didn't donate very much. But we do what we can."

"You don't need to apologize at all," I said. "It's wonderful. I'm so glad I could come."

"You also know about the upstairs synagogue?"

"Is it open for visitors?"

She smiled. "You're in luck. But only for another hour." She stepped away when another, more irate visitor, demanded she answer his question.

I left the room and walked upstairs. What awaited me were the remnants of one of the oldest city synagogues in all its haphazard glory. To my left was the ark, half-open with a Torah scroll peeking through; a thin layer of dust covered the wooden pews, and a display to my right held toys donated by the area schools. It had been a very long time since I'd stepped inside the premises of any sort of synagogue, and I hadn't given much thought to praying lately. But suddenly, I was gripped with the desire to face the ark, kneel down, and pray.

*I'm sorry*, my mind repeated over and over. *And I hope you'll understand.*

The fever passed and I stood up, mildly disoriented. A voice called out to me: "Miss? We're closing the museum soon."

I checked my watch. Six o'clock already. I dashed down the stairs, called a cab, and was back in my hotel room within twenty minutes. After a quick shower and change, I headed down to the bar, certain I was early. Deborah and the girls were well into their second round.

"You have a good afternoon then?" Hannah asked somewhat condescendingly. I noticed she was wearing new shoes, which pointed in odd directions and were decidedly unflattering.

"I got a good nap," I replied, trying not to stare at her shoes.

Too late. "Ferragamo. I never thought I'd find them in this ridiculous town."

"Stop it, Hannah," said Deborah, who'd swiveled herself in our direction, "We should get to Temple Bar. It's probably a madhouse by now."

It was. I'd warned Deborah, but even I couldn't imagine how many people had crowded themselves into this small area of bars, restaurants, and art galleries. I could barely hear what anyone was saying, and when at one point I tried to sit on a bench in the square's center, a shabby vagrant launched into a tirade about how he'd earmarked the seat for his own. I jumped away and followed the girls into Gogarty's, where Deborah had reserved the upper floor for her hen night needs.

Once we'd settled into our seats, Adele took out the tiara, Hannah brought out the lingerie, and a waiter appeared with cocktails. The chattering got louder and the gossip got nastier by the time Deborah quieted us all with a challenge.

"It's my last big weekend out and I'm with the girls I love most. But before I get married, I have to purge myself of all the shit I used to do as a single girl—"

"You're still single!" Carol yelled out.

"Barely, and besides, it'll be so much nicer when I'm married and I can boss you lot around."

Deborah giggled, and we joined in to humor her, even though it really wasn't all that funny.

"So in the spirit of things, we're all going to play a game called Confession."

"I've never heard of that," I said.

"That's because I just made it up. But it'll be great. So, each of you tell us something you've never revealed before, then drink your whole cocktail."

The rest of us glanced around nervously. Deborah was obviously pissed out of her tree, but this was a bit much.

"Well? Who's going to go first?"

Adele sat up in her chair. "Oh, all right. I shagged two blokes at the same time in uni."

Laura cackled. "How was it?"

Adele downed her drink. "Bloody painful!"

Everybody laughed, and the tension lifted.

Laura then proudly confessed to skimming a few thousand quid from her boss over the last couple of years. "But you've met him," pointing to Hannah and Carol, "so you see why. He's a complete tosser."

They nodded, and Laura drank up.

Carol's confession was hardly anything, just some bit about shoplifting. The only surprise was where and how much.

"Harrods? A five-thousand-pound sweater?" Deborah's eyes nearly popped out. "But how did you get away with it?"

Carol shrugged. "Dunno, but it wasn't so hard. Too nerve-wracking, though, and I wouldn't do it again." She looked down and fingered her sleeve. Seeing that, we all drank.

Hannah put down her glass angrily. "You lot make me fucking sick."

"What?" we chorused.

"You make me absolutely ill! Confessing all these horrendous things. You're all just play-acting anyway. You wouldn't know what something horrible is if you stared it in the face!"

Hannah's own had changed from red to purple.

"It's confession time, and I'll tell each and every one of you something, oh yes I will. Adele, you're a malicious cow who'd stab every one of us in the back if you could. And probably has. Remember David?"

Adele's face paled.

"Oh, yes bet you thought I'd never find out. You sorry little bitch. And then you, Carol, always stealing my work, passing it off as your own, and then getting better marks!"

Hannah stood up. "Now, I don't have much to say to you, Laura, but that you'd admit so happily to stealing money from someone who you set me up with? That you said time and again would be a good match for me? Why the fuck would I want to date someone like that, then?"

"I . . . I . . ." Laura stammered helplessly.

"And as for you, Andrea, you're simply nothing. No drive, no personality. I mean, why are you here? Because of Deborah's charity, that's why. Because you're just the poor fucking pseudo-relation who grew up on the wrong side of town and always got the scraps. Deborah's not your friend, she just pities you. Like the rest of us."

I couldn't move. It hurt to hear what I'd long suspected was the truth, especially broadcast for the entire bar.

"And then there's the would-be bride. Ha, that's what you think. Well, I've got a surprise, because it's time you knew the truth about Sam and what an utter wanker he is."

All of us sat on the edge of our seats, looking between Hannah and Deborah.

"Do you know he's tried to pull each and every woman sitting here? In some cases, he's actually succeeded. In fact, thanks to your dear fiancé, I'm going to have to get a fucking procedure when I get home from this sorry excuse for a party."

"You fucking bitch!" Deborah leaned across the table and would have punched Hannah if Laura hadn't caught her arm in time. "I never want to see any of you again!" Hannah threw the remains of her drink on the table and stormed out of the bar.

Deborah sat down shakily, trying to get her bearings. "Can someone get me another fucking drink?"

The night somehow continued, though the party feeling was long gone. After a while, Adele turned to me and asked half-heartedly if I had anything to confess.

I thought of the last time I'd seen Sam, right before I was due to board the plane. I'd asked him to come over even though he was busy at work. He'd been nastier than ever, threatening to tell Deborah all sorts of lies about me that would irrevocably ruin our friendship, hurling all sorts of awful insults at me. I couldn't help it. I grabbed the nearest thing I could to shut him up. It wasn't till he'd fallen to the ground, blood gushing out of his head, his eyes fixed in a stricken expression, that I realized what had happened. I had to act fast, especially as the cab I'd called would be arriving at any moment. Thankfully, so were the garbage collectors.

"No, not a thing," I said, and finished the remains of my cocktail.

# THE MAN FOR THE JOB
BY GARY PHILLIPS

No, how the hell could I be Wilson Pickett?"

"Oh, right. Sorry," the square mumbled as I stepped out of the cab. He went down the street the way he'd been heading when he stopped to ask me that bullshit.

"You sure this is where you want me to let you?"

"Ain't no sweat, man, I can handle it." I peeled off some bills and handed them to the driver. On the backseat was a folded newspaper and an article about that bald chick, the singer, Shanay, Sinbad, whatever the fuck, and how she'd joined some kind of Catholic cult and was calling for the Pope to renounce Beelzebub. Hilarious.

"Enjoy your stay, sir." He touched his cap and put his hack in gear. The car was just like the kind I'd seen roving around London, only there weren't as many of them here. You'd think they'd be stacked up at the hotel I was staying at, but the doorman hipped me to hoof over to O'Connell Street, where I found some lined up.

I snuggled my upturned collar closer to my neck and put the zipper of my leather jacket all the way up. When you got the crawlies like I had, everything is like constant heated pins poking from beneath your skin. Plus the goddamn cold, which I wasn't a fan of to begin with—gloomy weather was all up in my ass. I looked across a section of the park and could see the projects, or *estates* as they called them over here, just beyond.

Walking head down, hands tucked away, I knew deep inside but wouldn't fess up that I was two steps from being certified a fool. I could have been back in my comfortable hotel room, hands roaming all over Molly, Mary, or whatever the fuck was the name of the honey who'd started conversing with me in that pub after the game at Lansdowne.

"I've seen you play before," she said, her liquid browns steady on me.

I'd been giving her and a couple of her girlfriends the glance. They'd started whispering and giggling to each other after me and some of the others from the Dragons and the Claymores had strolled into the joint. The teams had come to Dublin to play an exhibition game at the stadium normally used for rugby and soccer. The stands weren't nearly as full for us as they would be for their own games, but the curiosity factor and that football, my kind of football, involved its own slamming and swearing got some of the natives out to see us. What the fuck, slappin' heads was slappin' heads.

And where you had muscular dudes grappling and tearing at each other, you had the type of woman who dug that kind of action—and not just to watch.

"When was that?" I said, moving to give her space at the bar. She leaned in.

"In Chicago. I lived there for a while. Had a job selling dog products."

"Dog products?"

"Flea-control solutions, chewy treats, that sort of rubbish."

I liked her toothy smile. Well, okay, I also liked the fact she had some guns straining that sweater she was wearing. Those bad boys were calling my name. But damn, she knew I was looking. She was too. "So you saw me on TV?"

"Live and in color," she said, assessing me up and down

like a coach figuring out if I was first-string or pine-rider. "Soldier Field. The Falcons against the Bears, before they were in the Central Division. You had two touchdowns for Atlanta." She paused, considering something, then said, "I believe you shook your arse at the crowd after that second one."

I gave her my gee-whiz Urkel bit. Babes like a mothafuckah to be self-effacing and shit. "Just trying to keep the fun in the game. Say did we—?"

"No, Zelmont, we didn't. All your women blur in your mind, do they?" She'd lit a cigarette and let the smoke float between us.

"It's not that, it's just, you know, when you're on the road during the season, shit just gets jumbled. 'Course, it's not like I'd forget you."

She knew it was bullshit, but it wasn't as if we were carrying on a romance like in one of them whack Merchant Ivory flicks I'd been forced to watch once. She knew the score.

And not an hour later, we were doing it freestyle in my room and I had my hands and lips all over her gorgeous ta-tas.

"I know this is going to sound off," I said later as we lay in bed, my hand rubbing her firm, what she'd call it? *Arse.* Hilarious.

"You're mad for me and want me to journey to your mansion in America with ya?" She said it in that kind of exaggerated Irish accent they used to do in those old black-and-whites where some stooped-over gray-haired dame played Jimmy Cagney's mother.

"Right," I said, gently squeezing one of her breasts, getting a moan out of her. She put her hand on mine. "Do you know where to cop some crack? Get some, I mean."

She laughed down in her throat. "Good thing I was in the States. Over here, *crack* means to fart and *the craic* means, well, means the good life. Which," and her amber eyes crinkled at the edges, "I guess is a kind of way of looking at it. Though lately that slang has found its way here, meaning what you mean."

I had no goddamn idea what the fuck she was talking about. I was needing, but had enough sense to know it was best not to go off and probably screw up what might be my only connection, and my only chance of doing the nasty again before I had to light out tomorrow.

She reached across me for the phone on the night stand, those wonderful titties mashing against my chest. "Let me make a few calls, darling."

And that's how I found myself staring, confused, at a sign. I figured the burning in my head had bored a hole in it and the crack cravings had me seeing mirages and what not. But then I remembered that Connolley, our backup quarterback, had been over here before to see some cousins and had mentioned that it wasn't unusual to see signs in Gaelic.

I sniffed, resisting the urge to scratch my itching, the invisible ants marching up and down my arms in sneakers with spikes. I tried to get rid of the image of hundreds of those tiny pincer jaws taking little chunk after little chunk out of my flesh. There was a sign in English just to the left of the Irish one, but the only reason I'd stopped was not to locate myself, but to get psyched. I was on a field I hadn't played on before, and had better be on my J.

Maura, yeah, that was her name, had told me that this place, Ballymun, was going through renovations. There was a main street running through the middle with brown and gray buildings on either side, and three tall main towers standing out. I didn't grow up in the projects but had been in more than a few in my time for one reason or another. Lately, though, it had been for the reason I was here now after being given my walking papers from the NFL for failing a random drug test, and getting bounced to the European league.

And it ain't like I was 24-7 on the pipe. I wasn't no weak-kneed dope fiend. It was just that my gimpy hip had been giving me fits again and I'd been hiding that precious detail from the docs. But if I asked for more than the usual allotment of painkillers, they'd know something was up. Hell, if you played ball for more than two years you just naturally needed some kind of legal narcotic cocktail to dull the constant throb from that sprained ankle that never had much of a chance to heal, or the tingle you never lost in your hamstring when you had to cut sharp down field. That was expected. The league's croakers knew what to give you for that shit, that was the ordinary.

But my on-again, off-again hip had started to pain me something fierce after I'd been tackled by this wheat-smellin' Russian fuck playing for the Monarchs two weeks ago in Wembley Stadium. Bad enough after that I'd started cutting the pain with crack, knowing it would hype the demand in me if I wasn't cool, and I could be the monkey dancing on the string again.

The fuck? Enough of that inspecting myself humbug. This wasn't no excursion to some all broads college with me working to get some muff diving professor and her prize pupil back with me to my room. Had to stay on point. I crossed behind a bulldozer on the low end of a mound of torn-down brick and wood and glass. There were a couple of figures moving over the mound, picking at this and lifting that in their search for plumbing pipes or porcelain to sell, I assumed.

I went past them and, checking the directions Maura had written for me, found the doorway I was looking for in the night. Not too surprisingly, there were some kids bivouacked in front of the building I'd been told to find. A couple of them were passing a joint and another was bopping to a boom box blazing a Tupac number, "Dear Mama." The aroma of their chronic drifted to me as I got close. Their blunt popped and sizzled, too many seeds in the cheap shit they were toking on.

"Hey," one of the kids said, spying me as Shakur growled, "I reminisced on tha stress I caused, it wuz hell huggin' on my mama from a jail cell."

"You a boxer, are you, mistah? Come to show us hooligans how to put our energies and urges to good use?" He did a quick flurry, hands and feet movin' and grovin' all the time, his eyes never leaving mine.

The others cracked up. The oldest of them couldn't have been over thirteen. Since yesterday it had been hard as Chinese chess for me to understand their accents. But now with the jones all over me like poison ivy, I was getting every word.

To the one, they all looked hungry. Not for a burger so much as that something they couldn't get growing up around here. Say what you want about anything else, but that was a condition I knew something about, 'cause it was how I'd come up in South Central L.A., even if I never did live in the projects.

"Gotta do some business." I flashed a ducat.

"Yeah?" the one who'd called me a boxer said. "Like 'em young, do you?"

"Sound like I'm cooing like Michael Jackson?" Not that I believed for a second these little shits wouldn't have taken me around the corner and laid a busted chair leg or rusted muffler upside my head in a heartbeat. I pressed the money into the kid's chest and he took hold of it. I pointed at the door behind him.

He snorted and, making a show like he was Jeeves, stepped aside, bowing and indicating for me to come forward. What a surprise, the door wasn't locked, and I entered the tower called Pearse, whoever the hell that was.

As the door closed behind me, my radar bumpin' in case one of them got a notion, I heard a *clop-clop*. I looked back through the safety glass and got sight of another kid in a watchcap and torn windbreaker galloping up to the others on a spotted nag. The horse's belly was sagging, the hind legs barely thicker than my arms, but damned if those kids didn't gather around it, petting and nuzzling the sad beast. Maybe they'd use the scratch I gave them to feed the thing rather than waste it on weed. Yeah, maybe.

I went up the stairs; the hallways were pretty clean and there were few busted lights considering it was public housing. I got to the fourth floor, an older lady all bundled up coming at me from the opposite direction, humming a tune. She lifted her head and then stopped singing. Her eyes went wide and she breathed all funny 'cause she wasn't sure what to make of me prowlin' about.

"What's this then?" she said as I stepped past. "You going undercover for the Gardaí?" She smelled of cigarettes and crushed flowers, and I finally got to the door I'd been directed to after Maura had made her third call.

"Now, mind you, you're an able lad, Zelmont," Maura had said, her hand down between my legs, "but you want to stay sharp, right? They'll be more scared of you, what with you being big and black and delicious"—she kissed me—"but they grow them tough over there too, right? Just because this isn't the

South Side or Harlem doesn't mean they'll all curl up and cry."

"Thanks, baby," I'd said, kissing her back. "You just order up a roast beef sandwich or potato pancakes or whatever the hell y'all eat over here from room service, and I'll be back soon for round two."

"You better," and she put some flutter in her lids while she locked her hand around my johnson, sliding her grip up and down its growing length. But I had the cravings so bad I didn't let her finish and left her snug under the blankets and me flicking icicles off my nose.

"What?" came a voice from inside the apartment after I knocked on number 435 a second time.

"Ian said I was cool." That was the name Maura told me to give.

"Did he now?" I didn't hear any feet scuffling.

I felt like hitting the door with the dull end of my fist to let him know I wasn't fuckin' around, but didn't want to jump wrong on turf I was clearly out of my element in. "Look here, I don't want to conduct my business in the street." A pensioner from the next door apartment was glaring at me. She wasn't going nowhere until I did.

"Who did you say?"

Fuck. "Ian. What? I talk like I got feathers in my mouth? Open this mothafuckah up, man, c'mon. I got the cheddah," I spat close to the wood. "Got dollars if you want."

The door hinged back. "Oh, well, that's different then, isn't it?"

I couldn't see much of the room beyond and didn't much care. I pushed through, if only to keep the old girl from giving me more of her vulture's stare. She was getting on my nerves, which were already about to shoot out of my pores, tingling as my sweat dripped over their raw ends.

"You a long way from home, my brother."

"You ain't never lied." The one who'd opened the door was lanky, with a dainty potbelly like you saw on cats who appreciated their apple pop tarts too much. He wore a pullover shirt and pants made out of cotton so goddamn thin I wondered how he didn't freeze his nuts off when he went out in them. He was barefoot but had on a plaid snap-brim hat pulled low over longish hair.

"And you're in need, yeah?"

"That's right." We'd each taken a step back from the other. I knew I could take his skinny ass, just like I knew it wasn't only me and homeboy in this crib. Which wasn't jacked up—no holes in the wall, the furniture, while there wasn't much of it, wasn't busted up, and there were no panes missing from the windows. There was even a TV on low with that big-headed Al Gore on it answering questions about him getting his campaign for the Dems nomination underway.

"So what is it you want, sir?" He smiled, lifting his chin some even though he was pretty much my height.

I was holding a few folded bills. "What I want is some crack."

He cocked his head to one side.

"But I'll settle for some snow," I said, putting a finger to the side of my nose and sniffing. Maura had explained to me that rock cocaine wasn't that big over here like it was in London, but that I should be able to purchase some flake. I figured at the hotel I could find some ammonia and cook it down to the shit I wanted.

"Ah, well, you've come to the right place, my American friend." He made to take the money from my hand.

"Don't play me for no chump," I said, holding onto them benjamins like I was guarding grandma's teeth

He snapped his fingers. "Right you are. Barbara," he said, adjusting his hat. To my left, where I guess the bedroom was, a thick-shouldered but pretty-in-a-rough-way chick with dirty blond hair stepped into the doorway. She had on tight jeans and a loose shirt, heavy boots on her feet. She jiggled a plastic baggie with a measure of white stuff in it. Maybe she figured I'd make like Rover and start panting. Did I look that messed up?

"Hello," she said, being too friendly.

"Hi yourself." The way I was positioned, I could drop her boyfriend with a kick and spin, and catch Barbara just right on the jaw. Between the two of them, she'd be the one to give me trouble. She didn't move and neither did he. I unzipped my jacket to give my arms more freedom.

I walked toward her, one hand out and the other extending the bills. Maura had told me I should be able to get a hit for roughly forty-five American. She took the money and gave me the shit. I opened the bag, worried the powder was more yellow than white. I sampled a taste on my pinkie, my face scrunching up.

"This is heroin."

"Yeah, what of it?"

"Did I say I wanted H?"

"Look, Sonny Jim, that's the way it is, yeah? You come for your high, get *mellow*, and we're done." The dude was peddling backward, no doubt to fetch his persuader.

I was hurtin' but I wasn't gonna be bitched up, especially by some foreigners. Naw, that kind of shit don't happen to me. "Give me back my scratch. We ain't got a deal." I tossed the bag on a chair.

"We're not Dunnes, understand? All sales final." The chick stood her ground, ready to throw down. She squinted at me.

"You're that hard man, aren't you? The one that was

mouthing off on the telly last night about how you'd come to the land of Lucky Charms to show us how to play real football."

Usually I got a twang in my dick when a broad recognized me. Not tonight. "My money, huh?"

"You say he's famous?" the man asked, now positioned next to a low cabinet with a lamp on it. "On a team, is he?"

"Yeah," she said, her tongue cavorting. "And he used to be something over in the States."

"Still am, baby." Now these mothafuckahs were clownin' me.

"Right, he's worth something to somebody," the man said, as he whipped open the cabinet door and reached inside for his gat. But I'd already turned, stepped, and leaped. I plowed into him and we knocked the lamp over, breaking it apart, making the room shadowy. The chick was also in motion and she jumped on my back, rockin' and sockin'.

"Spence, for fuck's sake, get him down!" she hollered, as I bent my arm back and got it around her neck and threw her off me and into her boyfriend. Problem was, she wasn't without reflexes and she'd grabbed hold of me and took me with her. It was like some kind of fucked-up Abbott and Costello movie with the three of us wrasslin' and yankin' on each other.

I got a grip on Spence's upper arm to keep him from planting that piece, which wasn't much of one, in my grill, while Broom Hilda rode me like Lafite Pincay and punched me good in the lower back and kidneys. I pushed back to the wall to put my weight on Barbara and still keep a grip on Spence. I managed to tag him with an uppercut, jarring his eyeballs in their sockets.

"Come on, be fair, we'll share what we make on you," the blonde said.

I couldn't figure out whether to laugh or cry. Wasn't no one in the NFL or Pop Warner, for that matter, 'bout to put together a buffalo nickel to ransom my sorry self. We tumbled to the floor all tangled up.

I was hitting Spence again, who was straddling me, but homegirl, who was underneath me, got her arm around my neck and hammer-locked the shit out of my Adam's apple. I had to let go of the man and he crashed the muzzle of his gun down against my temple. But like I said, it wasn't much of a gun, it was a derringer, like what Jim West used to pop out of his sleeve to make Dr. Loveless shit in reruns of the *Wild Wild West* TV show.

For a hot minute the black lights had me, but I couldn't let 'em take me under.

"That's it," I heard her say, as if she were deep in the ground below me. "Put him under."

Spence clubbed at my head again, but I got my shoulder up and that took most of the blow. I drove an elbow into her rib cage and that got her gasping and sputtering. I shook loose from Barbara and came up, arms wrapped around Spence, taking him over in a tackle. I was quick enough that by the time he tried to level his pea shooter, the back of his head made contact, loudly, with the thinly carpeted floor, dazing him.

Girlfriend got her arms around my legs and put her choppers into me like my thigh like it was prime rib. "Fuck!" I screamed, and used my fist as a club to work at the base of her neck. That got her jaw open and I straight right-crossed the broad, making blood spray.

Spence fired his derringer but I'd grabbed the hefty chick for a shield and he'd pulled his aim up, shooting the ceiling. We were back on the floor and I lashed out with my foot, catching Spence alongside his cheek. He bowled over and, shoving the woman away, I jumped on him and commenced to wail on the chump like he'd stolen from my baby's mama. He lay still and I got up, putting the derringer in my jacket pocket. That toy wasn't much of a threat, but I might need it.

"Come on," I said to her, a jagged piece of the busted lamp steady in my hand, on her eyeball.

"You gonna have your way with me?" There didn't seem to be a lot of fear in her voice. Maybe Barbara the blonde was sizing me up to be a replacement for Spence.

She got off the floor and I made her give me their stash. It was H and some marijuana. I had a plane to catch tomorrow afternoon and what was the chance I'd be able to parlay this stuff into the coke I needed before then? Fuck it, though. They had to offer decent recompense for inconveniencing me. I fooled with the idea of doing Barbara—big-legged women had serious effects on me. She was giving me that look. Of course, there was Maura waiting for me at the hotel and the chronic would cut some of my hype. Of course, pussy was pussy . . .

She started unbuttoning her shirt. I watched a thin trail of sweat dribble between her braless breasts. She smiled, showing overlapping teeth.

I uppercut her, dropping her like a sack of cement. "I can't shake the feeling that you'd slip a blade between my ribs just for fun."

I left her blinking at me, sitting on the floor. I stepped over the beaten Spence and left with my plastic bag of thrills.

Back at the hotel, the fight and fatigue had spent some of my craving. With a little weed, some blasts of the scotch I'd bought earlier, and hopefully mucho head from my visitor, that should keep me tight.

"Darling," she said. She was laying down, a patch of light across her from the slightly open door to the bathroom.

"They didn't have any crack."

"Oh, don't give out. Come over here and I'll make it up to you." She squirmed, that gorgeous ass waiting for me to do something to it.

"You better." I already had my jacket off.

I was slipping out of my shoes when she came from beneath the covers. The gun she had on me was *the business*, as they say over here. Not at all like that pop gun of Spence's

"That's my lad." She got out of bed, fully dressed. She grabbed the shit I'd brought back, me sitting there frowning on the end of the bed, watching her, the gun dead on me. "I'd hoped those eejits would get *dumb*, I think the term is, right, baby? Try to cheat me, would they?"

"And what would have happened if they'd jammed me up?"

She patted my face, doing a kissy thing with her lips. "I had no such worries. You're too much of a stud to let them do that."

She was at the door, looking back, halfway into the empty hallway. "I told you I've been following your career, Zelmont. I know all about your problems with drugs, how you got exiled over here. And like all of you pampered sportsmen, you can't imagine a woman not swooning because you have sleek muscles and a lovely dick. Which you do have. You lived up to your reputation."

"For being stupid."

"No. I'd say you're too much a slave of your appetites. That's going to get you in real trouble someday, love, if you're not careful. But for my purposes, you were certainly the man for the job." She left, closing the door quietly behind her.

I curled up on top of the bed, the crack crawlies convulsing my body. I downed half the damn bottle of booze and sweated it out as fast as I took it in. Somewhere around 6:00 in the morning I got to sleep, and at 9:00 I woke up and couldn't get my eyes shut anymore. I cleaned up and was ready when the bus came to get us for the airport.

Walking through the facility, I spotted a dude reading a *Time* magazine. There was an article about an expansion football team starting up in Los Angeles called the Barons. L.A. hadn't had a pro team since the Raiders left. Now that was something. Maybe I had one more chance at the bright lights, just one more shot. Could be last night was a kind of warning.

Get it together, Zee, and there could be the roaring crowds and sweet honeys again, the smack-talkin' interviews on ESPN and the million dollar endorsement deals pimping glorified grape juice. Yeah, shit yeah. I was going to show Maura and all of them, I was the man for the job. Fuuuck . . .

# THE NEW PROSPERITY
BY Patrick J. Lambe

T he first thing you have to get used to working in the IT field is all the bloody Pakis. They're stinking up the cubicles of Ireland with their curry stench. I know they're not all Pakis, they're not all angling for their seventy veiled virgins in Jihadville. Some of them are Hindus. Some of them talk with refined Cambridge accents. Some of them will spring for a round or get their feed on in a chipper. A generation or two hence, I wouldn't doubt they'll be praying to Mohammed and Ganesh in Gaelic.

Megan says I shouldn't be so hard. She says Ireland went out to the world, now it's time for the world to come to Ireland. She might have a point. It's been a few years since I've been on the dole. It's not like any jackeen who wants a job is left out. Everyone seems to be working with the new prosperity. We all have to eat, even the bloody wogs and Pakis. Can't accuse me of not doing my part, I was feeding one of them: my boot.

Steel-toed solution.

"A race of bloody poets," the Englishman says. He'd just walked in, got a look at me as I'm cleaning blood off my boot with a rag dipped in a pint of seltzer water, after me mate Freddy and me had finished our jig on the wog. I'd thought I was done, but got a touch of last-minute inspiration, turned heel on the way back to the pub, and kicked him two more times, "One for Molly Maguire and one for the Queen Mother." Freddy got a kick out of that one, doubled over laughing.

"Fucking blow in, shouldn't have been trying to pull a Bloom on us. He should be sticking his little brown stick into his own kind," I say, as I replace the rag with a shotglass, tilt the Jameson down. I winked at Megan when I said it. She was a beauty all right, if not too discerning. I'd often thought about going a round or two with her. Freddy had told me kissing the blarney stone would be more sanitary. He then educated me as to what the lads are up to when the tourists aren't around. Apparently it's the biggest cock manger in the whole country.

"Bad form, lads. The Indian fellow works with me. He's a friend of mine. There'll be consequences."

Fred's bloodlust was still up, but I put my arms around his shoulder before he took a step toward the Englishman; ordered another round of the black, with a Jameson chaser. Something about the Brit's eyes. I think he lived west side, Tallaght maybe. I felt he was almost one of us, despite the Imperial legacy. He'd been drinking here at the Clannagh for nigh onto a year now, by my best estimate. He'd worked with Fred and me for a few months at the financial institution, babysitting the computers running the new prosperity, feeding off Dublin's newly ripened teat. A few steps up from the dole, just like the rest of us.

Besides, he had a Celtic surname, as far as I can recall. Figured him for a county boy come back to see how his grandfather lived, before he emigrated to Liverpool to stick rivets in the side of the Imperial Navy. I'd bet he knelt down and genuflected in the direction of the Pope five times a day, just like the rest of the lads throwing back Guinness and Jameson at the pub.

"Fucking wanker. Why don't ye go back across the sea. We don't need you stirring the pot over here," Fred said.

He should be one of the last to speak, Fred. He's a fucking culchie. Blowed in from County Cork, I think. His company is barely tolerable at the best of times. I wouldn't have anything to do with him if he didn't have a throat as often as I did.

The Brit downed his pint in one long, continuous draught, catching my eye the whole time. "There'll be consequences," he repeats.

"Call the Gardaí if you've a mind," I said.

The Gardaí had better things to do than worry about a Punjabi bleeding a Ganges of blood into the gutter. The reason me mate and I were so pissed is because the bank we worked at turned us out early. Couple of lads in Balaclavas had robbed the place; gotten away with a boatload of euros. The cunts worked over the narrowback who had repatriated to guard the stash. The Yank had reclaimed his Irish citizenship, only to have the shit kicked out of him with hurley sticks. Freddy and me had gotten a raise out of that. Score one for Ireland.

The Englishman turned and left.

"I'm shaking in me boots," Fred says. "Threatened by a scut who can't hold down a job in this economy." I remembered then, the Brit had been fired. Incompetence, I think. They'd been so desperate for bodies they'd offered to retrain him. He told them to fuck off, and went back on the dole.

I must have been buckled because I found myself in Megan's gaff a bit after the holy hour. She was a fine thing, Megan. She had the map of Ireland painted on her face, and since I was going in without me slicker, sweet baby Jesus willing, I'd paint a map of the Hebrides all over her sweet belly, in a shade of white paler than her skin.

I don't know why she took me home. She'd never fancied me before I defended her wee bit of honor. Maybe it was a deeper need, or maybe she really did like me. I stopped thinking about it as soon as I got a glimpse of her pubes.

I love Dublin in the rain, the drops bouncing off the bricks, the stabbers looking like boats riding little rivers between the cobblestones; reminds me of my history lesson. Some of the Vikings, tired of rape and pillage, took a fancy to the place where the River Poddle joined the Liffey; Dubh linn, *Black pool* in the old language. They'd settled down, married some of the local women, and started trading with the painted inland chiefs.

I felt bad about pulling a legger on Megan, but I thought kindly of her, a heavy blanket between the chill predawn morning and her fine pelt.

She'd surprised me the night before, when we tangled up in each other after we'd done with the rasher. She'd the accent and the attitude, had her pegged for skanger, but she was a bogger, slipped out of Sligo a little after her fourteenth birthday and managed to stay two footfalls away from the whorehouse steps since. I felt like I was the only jackeen left in the whole pissing city.

That is, till the hurley stick took my legs out from under me. I figured it was a couple of local lads looking for a quick score. Then I thought better of it.

It was the worst beating of my life, and not on account of the pain. A couple of Manchester boys and a Yank had turned my piss to blood a few years ago when I was on the piss after a football match. I'd limped around for a few months after that one. I'd probably shrug this one off in under a week. Still, I prayed for a two bulb, or even a wasp to save me from the humiliation.

The fucking wog and the sasancach used hurley sticks on me. Judging by the dried flecks of blood mingling with my fresh batch, I'd say they were the same pieces of Irish ash they'd used to work over the narrowback. The fucking wankers had probably paid for them with euros.

# LONELY AND GONE

BY DUANE SWIERCZYNSKI

Caidé an scéal?

Conas atá tu?

Oh, not Oirish, are you? Funny. You've got the pale skin, dark hair, the whole Gaelic vibe 'bout you.

Me? Spent a lot of time here and there. A lot of it here.

No, not literally *here*, in this pub. Nice place, though, innit? *Trés* Victorian.

Hey, let a girl buy you a drink.

Yeah, I'm foukin' serious. Fancy a pint?

Oh. A Scotch man. A thousand pardons. Allan, could you pour this handsome devil here a Johnnie Walker black? To match his hair.

It's a joke, boyo.

You're a serious one, aren't you?

Let me take a wild foukin' guess: You're American. And your wedding ring's in your carry-on, right?

Yeah, sure I'll watch your drink. I've got Allan here to keep me company.

That was quick.

Yeah, sarcasm. Bingo.

Ah, just drink up. Your ice is already melting. Tell me about yourself.

Hi, Jason. I'm Vanessa. Glad we covered the basics.

No, you first. I insist. I'll get to me in a little while.

*Sin scéal eile?*

Ah. Knew you were a customer-relations man, Jay. I could just tell.

Ever scale the museum steps—like in *Rocky?*

Nah, never been. I'm sure I'll make it there eventually.

Yes, yes.

Hmm.

Very interesting. Really. Would I lie to you, Jaybird?

Oh me?

Me, I've got a plane to catch in exactly fourteen hours. Which means I've got time to kill. And to be perfectly blunt, Jason, I'd like to spend it with you.

Which is why I poisoned your drink . . .

Uh-huh.

As you Americans say: *deadly.*

Whoops.

Was it something I said?

*Tá tú air ais.*

Means, "I knew you couldn't cut it abroad."

It usually takes a few minutes to sink in.

Yeah, it'd be easy to think I'm crazy. Or that I've got a seriously sick sense of humor. But part of you is wondering, right? Wondering if there's a tiny chance that I'm serious?

Jason, *mo ghrá*, I'm completely serious.

Hand on the Holy Book, I poisoned your drink.

Nasty stuff, too. I'm not going to bore you with the precise chemical compound—you probably didn't like chemistry in secondary school in Philadelphia, did you?

Didn't think so.

Well, let's just cut the shit—in about twelve hours, you're

going to be bleeding out yer eyes. Your skin's going to turn red and slough off your muscles. It'll start with an itch. Then you'll itch all over. It'll drive you crazy. And you'll scratch. And you won't be able to stop.

Yeah. Weapons-grade.

I know it's easy for you to think that.

Such a mouth on you.

Walk out of this bar and you'll never see Philadelphia again.

They're called *gardaí* here. Guards. And they can't help you.

No one can.

Only me.

Hey, Jaybird . . . pub closes at midnight!


An hour and forty-five minutes. That's a new record.

You started itching, didn't you?

Oh, sit down. I'll explain everything. Almost.

Want another drink?

Swear to Christ, I'll leave it be.

Suit yourself.

Here it is, Jaybird. I've been poisoned, too. No, not with the same stuff. Something else. Something worse. If I'm alone, my heart will stop. And my brain will burst.

Oh, I wish it were a bloody poem. No, I mean it literally. If I don't have someone within six feet of me at all times, I will die.

What's that?

Look around you. We're in a crowded pub on Dame Court. Plenty of people. Until midnight. Until I have to leave and go for a walk down Dame Lane. If I'm not with someone like you, I'll be one dead dame.

Gallows humor is my specialty. It's on my CV. Right after biochemistry.

Nah, I never did tell you, did I? Well take a wild foukin' guess.

Uh-huh. U.S. of A.

I work here. The Celtic Tiger's been roaring. We've got all kinds of labs.

More on the research end, but yeah. You've got it.

Ah, I know you're humoring me. But that's okay. As long as you humor me for the next twelve hours.

No way, huh?

Okay, then. Piss off.

Really, I'll poison some other handsome devil. Have a nice flight. Hope your bride doesn't mind a closed casket.

*Bí curamach.*

Allan, I'd suck a dick for another pint, so how about it?

Back now, are you?

Your skin must be driving you mad by now.

Me? You want to know about me?

Ah, you're just looking for the antidote. Nothing more. Maybe a blowjob before you die. Yeah, well ask me arse, ye bollix. I'm desperate. Just not *that* desperate.

Yeah, I know what I said to Allan. It's an Oirish thing. Ironic exaggeration. You wouldn't understand.

Okay, fine, the antidote. We'll get to that. In a while. First you've got to hear my story. Don't worry, I'll give you the abridged version.

Look above you. Past the ceiling of this pub, deep into the clear Irish sky. Not as far as the stars. Just below. Can you see it? The spinning silver ball?

Humor me. Tell me you can see it.

Yeah, that spinning silver ball. The foukin' satellite.

Use your imagination, Jason, for fuck's sake. That's why God gave it to you.

Okay. You see it. Now picture this: biochemical triggers in my blood. You can make them silver, too, if you want. Little silver balls, swimming round my red and white cells. AIDS? I'd welcome AIDS. There's shit we can do 'bout AIDS. We can't do anything 'bout *this*. These little silver balls. Can you see them?

Good. Now imagine the big silver ball in the sky.

Yeah, the satellite, Jaybird.

That's the big silver ball that's fixed on the tiny silver balls in my blood. It needs six feet circumference to do its job, otherwise the big silver ball could kill innocent people. Besides me, hah hah.

Star wars.

Yeah. My lab's been busy the past twenty years.

So yeah, okay, if I were to get up from this bar stool and walk across Dame Court? You'd see me lovely body fall to the ground. Dead. Those silver balls are brutal. They grow spikes. In my heart. In my brain.

Jesus can't help me, but thanks for the sentiment anyway.

Who? Beats the royal fuck out of me. Maybe some jealous foukin' bastard in the lab. A jilted lover. A bored and horny bureaucrat. Fucked if I know. Maybe I should have given a ride. Suck some dick for science, right?

You can help me by staying with me. For at least eleven hours. That's when help will arrive, *le cúnamh Dé*. And the big silver ball won't be able to say shite about it. As long as you stay within six feet of me.

Oh, my hotel room? Just a few blocks away. I'm at the

Westbury. When I'm in Dublin, I make it a point to stay five-star. You've gotta see the bathroom.

Yes, that's where I have the antidote.

Aren't you going to hold my arm, *mo ghrá?*

Of course it's nice. What did you expect? We're in central Dublin, not foukin' Galway.

Stop asking. It's not important. What's important is you and me. Together. Tonight. Within six feet of each other, at all times.

You don't mind if I handcuff you to the bed, do you?

No, I wasn't exactly joking.

Mm!

Mmmmmm.

Well.

This is an unexpected development.

The handcuffs, wasn't it?

I do have them, swear to Christ. Right here in my bag. See?

Oh.

Mmmmm.

These turn you on, do they?

Oh, we're almost there.

It is a beautiful lobby, isn't it? Almost as beautiful as my lips, wouldn't you say?

Oh, the mouth on you.

Here we are. Push the *up* arrow, boyo.

What?

I wouldn't worry about that. The antidote doesn't matter. What matters is us. Together. Tonight. You, here with me. For . . . yeah, looks like eleven hours.

*Ding.*

Yes, Jason?

625. Why?

What are you—

*You snap the one cuff around her wrist and the other around the car rail. You watch her eyes widen as you step back.*

*And the doors close.*

*The frantic pounding and clanging. The wail of betrayal.*

*Then you swear you can sense it: the faint tremor just beyond the range of human hearing.*

*Because the wail has stopped.*

*No need to worry about that antidote. You knew she'd made it up. Her security clearance doesn't give her access to the hard stuff.*

*You unflip your cell. Dial the number that after a few security switches will connect you with a basement somewhere in Virginia. All you have to do is make this phone call and you can hop your plane home to Philadelphia. Just two words, and you've earned your paycheck.*

*"It works," you say.*

# ROPE-A-DOPE

BY CRAIG MCDONALD

Harcourt Street, a raucous downstairs bar: über meat market.

George has his eye on a woman—out of his league, but worst she can say is no.

And he knows this: Lonely women fear lonely weekends like death.

Friday, just after work. This, in his too-successful experience, is every lonely woman's hour of least resistance.

Pints are guzzled by lookers in little black dresses who've spent their days skirting the boundaries of "casual Friday" good taste—sweaters or jackets between them and stern warnings from sundry Human Resources Nazis.

George signals the gaffer, points at the woman alone at the table near the door.

The keep nods and half-smiles, says, "Russian Quaalude."

George Lipsanos scowls. "What the fuck kind of drink is that?"

The barkeep smiles and shrugs. "Obscure one: Frangelico, Bailey's, and vodka. Honestly? Had to look it up."

Impatient, George nods. "Send her a double."

Lipsanos watches. The bartender serves the sleek stranger the drink. Questioned, he stabs a thumb at George.

The woman raises an eyebrow, lifts her glass, and nods at George.

Lipsanos is headed her way before her first sip.

As he approaches, she shifts her legs—long legs, already crossed. Her right foot now slips behind her left leg's calf.

This woman was striking at thirty yards in dim light through a haze of cigarette smoke. At five feet, she's a leggy wet dream: mocking green eyes, dark hair . . . chiseled chin . . . natural rack, and good thighs on full display in her tight-black, fuck-me-now-and-hard! dress.

George thinks . . . *righteous, compliant sports fuck.*

Or she soon will be.

She smiles at him—a sultry, mocking mouth. She sips her freaky cocktail, says: "'Tis himself. Ah, but he didn't know my drink. Maybe doesn't bode well." Another sip, then, "You're not Irish."

George scowls, shakes his head: "No . . . I'm Greek." He shrugs. "Came to ride the Celtic Tiger. Get some of that Y-2K paranoia action." He omits the latest nuance: a lucrative leap to cyber-porn. Instead, George hefts his glass, butchering the pronunciation: *"Sláinte!"*

A husky chuckle. The woman smiles—deep dimples—and winks. "My father's from Glencoe. You know . . . the Highlands? He'd a toast, 'Here's to you, as good as you are. Here's to me, as bad as I am. And as bad as I am, and as good as you are, I'm as good as you are, as bad as I am.'"

George has trouble tracking that one. She drains her Russian Quaalude. She signals the bartender, raises her glass, and points at George.

She leans across the table, fingers tented, drawing elbows closer and deepening the dark, enticing valley between her high-riding breasts. "Guess I won't hold it against you, then . . . not knowing my drink."

"Yeah," George says, "that's good." He puts out his hand. "I'm George."

She squeezes his hand and sits back, breasts shifting under her dress. She tips her head to the side, dark hair slanting. "My name is the last thing on your mind. Let's be honest, huh, George? Names truly important?"

He feels some sense of firm footing returning. Cocky, he says, "Called out at the right moment? Yeah . . . means more than *Oh baby*."

Those dimples again. She sips her drink, points. "Gutsy, George. Joking about sex this early. Okay: You can call me Mell. Mell Mulloy."

He puts out his hand again, squeezes hers and doesn't let go—his thumb stroking the inside of her palm.

She says, "*George*. Hmm. Like the monkey, huh?"

"Say what?"

"The monkey . . . my favorite book as a kid, ya know? *Curious George?* The little chimp . . . man with the yellow hat?"

"Gotcha." George bites his lip . . . sips his drink. *Jesus*: Best steer clear of books with this woman . . . literature—not his territory. The last one went on and on about "Joyce" . . . guaranteeing he'd never read *that* bitch.

But the woman pushes: "Are ya, you know, curious . . . George?"

George's kidneys are burning. Should have hit the head before he sent the drink to her. He bounces his left leg. Tries to come up with some response to her question. He fingers the engraved Zippo in the pocket of his sports jacket, says, "You smoke?"

"Not anymore."

"Mind if I do?"

"Do it, George—secondhand smoke keeps me half-ass in the game."

George lies: "Gotta get it in before the ban, yeah? I'm out . . . gotta get myself a new pack."

He beelines for the men's room. He shoulders up between pissed, pissing punters and lets go, his left kidney burning . . . even aching.

The pain subsiding, he washes up and hits the cigarette machine. He buys a pack of Regals that he'll maybe get through in three or four weeks. He drops it in his pocket with the baggie of half-a-dozen tablets of Rohypnol—the "R2" that he figures to slip in Mell's drink when she has to hit the head.

But before that, he'll slip her the Ecstasy in his left pocket. *Yeah.*

The E and the "Rope"—a profoundly powerful one-two . . . no woman could sustain against it.

Mell has a fresh drink waiting for George when he returns to their table.

George slides into his chair—freshly stricken: that face, those tits, those long legs . . . thinking about those legs wrapped around his ass . . . about Mell's mouth, her sultry lips, groaning—and her not *remembering*—sucking.

"Drink up, George," Mell says. "They're gonna be playing our song in a minute."

Compliantly, George downs his double Jameson and accepts her hand.

They find an empty space on the dance floor and begin moving together, his crotch tight to hers—a slow dance to Mark Knopfler: "On Raglan Road."

George is dizzy.

And increasingly hard.

Mell clearly knows it too—stroking him through his sans-a-belt pants.

Punchy, his pants now a tent, George follows Mell back to their table. He doesn't really sit so much as he falls into his chair.

George is sweating—even a little nauseous.

Strike that: *really* nauseous . . . sweating like a pig. He had loaded nachos about 4 p.m. He thinks of the sour cream slathered on the chips, then thinks, *Jesus, it's food poisoning!*

But Mell has slipped off her right fuck-me stiletto, distracting George from his sour stomach. She's massaging his crotch with her stockinged foot. She says: "Don'tcha think it's time we go to your place? You do have a place, George?"

She stands . . . reaches under the table with her left hand and pulls up a big black bag—something between a large purse and a briefcase.

George takes her extended right hand, trailing her through the packed pub to the door. His head is swimming . . . *Jesus, didn't even need pills for the bitch . . . must be a fucking wild ride.*

The wet cold air is a fleeting respite, soothing him . . . sharpening his focus.

But the cab is too cozy. George mumbles his home address and slides into a void.

*In that void: polluted with conversation . . . Mell and the cabby— engaged in meaningless small talk. He just hears bits of some unfair barbs from Mell: "Poor George—he so can't handle his booze . . . full-on scuttered."*

*George would object if he could find his voice.*

He's cold.

George blinks his eyes, looks around.

*Jesus Christ!* Fucking naked and spread-eagled on his back on his own bed.

His hands are cuffed to the bed posts . . . ankles, ditto.

Mell's standing there at the foot of his bed, sneering in her slinky black dress.

"He has risen," Mell nods at George's still-hard cock.

"What the fuck is this?" George's tongue is thick and he hardly understands himself. He thinks he might vomit.

"Fecking caffler," Mell says, "you really have no idea what's going on?"

Groggy, George mutters, "Uh, *no* . . ."

The woman crosses her arms, feet spread wide. "Brill. Let me help: You're coming through a smallish dose of Rope—or Rohypnol . . . the original date-rape drug. If Valium was Superman, well, Rope is Superman's bigger, meaner older brother. But you know that, don'tcha, George?" She raises her hand—sheathed in a white latex glove—and his baggie of Rope flops down. Mell scowls, looking hurt. "Meant this evil shit for me, eh, Georgie?"

With her other rubber-gloved hand, the woman suddenly grasps George's erection and squeezes. George winces, willing himself soft. Surely in this circumstance, he'll go soft . . . but he stays hard. Maybe gets harder.

Mell says, "Hmm. No baz. Not appealing." She then adds, squeezing him again, "This wood of yours is the result of a Viagra knock-off. If you're online, you've probably gotten Spam e-mail offers for it. You'll stay hard at least another two hours, George . . . maybe three. You'll stay real hard, regardless of anything—hardness that could be confused for excitement. But, I jump ahead."

"What is this?" George sneers unconvincingly, hearing his dope-stoked drunkness in his slurred voice. "Fuck you doin', Mell?" Drool slides from the corner of his mouth. "These fucking drugs . . . they could fucking kill me."

The woman sits on the edge of the bed and shakes her head. "Stay easy. I'm a doctor. Know what I'm doing. And it was a half-dose of Rope. I wanted this talk with you."

A *doctor*. Now George is in full panic mode . . . Stories he always thought were urban myths about organ thefts . . . Pick up some chick . . . take her to a hotel . . . and then you wake up with a kidney missing . . . *Jesus fuck!* He blubbers, "You want my fucking kidneys."

A husky laugh. "If that was the game, you'd be in a tub of ice now with a hole in your back. Two, if I was really ruthless." Mell leans in now, searching his eyes. George thinks about screaming and maybe she senses it—she drives a fist into his solar plexus and he doubles up . . . chafing skin off his wrists and ankles . . . his mouth open, gasping for air. Suddenly, there's a rag in his mouth.

"You're done talking, forever. I asked you if names are important. Well, they are important, George. Here's a name for you: *Nora MacKiernan.* That name ring a bell?"

George shakes his head.

"Well, she remembered your name, George. You were dumb enough to use your real first name, just like you did with me. She remembered that Zippo of yours, with your initials. You doped her in that same bar I met you in. None of that made it nearly hard enough to find you. Four weeks, cruising the same five or six bars . . . and I found you back in the one where you drugged her.

"Nora MacKiernan was twenty-three, George. She was at that bar with irresponsible mates who were there to be laid and shamed her along after work. Nora was engaged. Would have wed next month. But you moved in. She was polite . . .

Nora was always polite."

The woman's eyes are drifting now, going sad and a little hard. George is breathing faster.

"You hit Nora, *my sister*, with Ecstasy, slipped her Rope . . . I know because I ran the rape kit and stomach pump at the hospital. And you gave her genital herpes, George. Those are fucking incurable. Nora's fiancé couldn't take it . . . broke their engagement. Nora couldn't take it, either . . . losing him . . . carrying your disease. Nora opted out. Wrists, razor . . . a warm bathtub. Suicide—very bad news in an old Catholic family."

Lipsanos shakes his head.

"Names are important, George." She rises now, sways across the room, and picks up her big black purse. She rummages. Mell turns, holding a hypodermic. She flicks it, squirts a little out—clear those air bubbles. She says: "My name is Ceara, and as even you have probably gathered, George, I wouldn't be sharing my real name with you now if there was any prospect of you ever leaving this room."

Mell—*Ceara*—perches again on the side of George's bed. She slowly crosses her legs. "Question was, how to make you really pay. I thought about that. I went to the personals . . . *Gáire*."

Ceara jabs George's thigh with the needle.

His eyes go wide and his muscles tense.

"Hush," Ceara says. "It's fine, George. Just a cocktail . . . blood-thinners . . . anti-coagulants." Her gloved hand on his penis again—still rock hard. "Shouldn't interfere with this."

The woman stands, slips off her latex gloves, and smoothes her short black dress over her thighs. She slips the needle and the gloves back in her big purse, then slings the bag over one shoulder.

"Gotta go, George. But, just so you know what's in store: I've been corresponding on your behalf for several days with a sado-masochistic she-he, deep into domination. You're into bondage. Some match, yeah? I've been stringing 'shim' along until I found you. Called him—her . . . *whatever*—a few minutes before you woke up. Quite soon, you and your righteous wood will be serving as bound *top* to his—her's . . . *whatever's*—enthusiastic *bottom*."

George is still reeling . . . dopey . . . scared . . . slow on the uptake: *Jesus, I have herpes?*

And this girl, *Nora* . . . couldn't remember her . . . but there had been a dozen since George found his Rope connection.

Ceara is framed in the doorway of his bedroom now. She tips her head to the side, shows him those dimples. "Last thing you should know, George."

George's eyes are wide, besieging.

"I told your soon-to-arrive last lover that you're also a *cutter*. Ya know what Angelina Jolie once said? 'You're young, in love, and you've got a knife . . . shit happens.' George, those blood-thinners will have you pumping like a world-class hemophiliac when your new friend cuts you. Once the initial slices are made, and the serious blood loss kicks in, well, it's not the worst death . . . almost languorous. Probably why Nora chose to take herself out that way."

Ceara blows George a kiss and backs out of his bedroom, humming "The Parting Glass."

George, spread-eagled, hard—panicked—thrashes wildly against his bonds, wrists and ankles sloughing more skin.

A short while later, he hears the door of his apartment open.

George closes his eyes and whimpers against his gag. *Sweet Jesus, Nora . . . I'm so fucking sorry.*

* * *

On Grafton Street, behind the bright red façade of the Temple Bar, Dr. Mell Mulloy sips her Russian Quaalude. Rain thrashes the windows. Positively bucketing. She savors George's final expression: *brónach*.

The herpes angle always sets their hearts hopping.

And poor imaginary *Nora*? Her *pièce de résistance:* Send the luckless bastards out on a mega guilt trip.

Finding the Rope on George made it sweeter still—so *so* fine to find a fellow predator . . . yummy, happy accident.

Mell checks her watch: Time for one more. But nothing elaborate. The personal-ad gambit takes time . . . and time is always a dangerous commodity.

So something simple is in order: Pick up another mark . . . dope him. Entice the sucker to his car or an alley for an ostensible jaw-job and shoot the fucker.

Then it is probably best to move on.

The Garda Síochána will soon start putting two and three or thirteen together.

Mell sips her drink and tips her head back, shaking loose her hair, lifting it off the back of her damp neck. Mell plucks an ice cube from her drink and rubs it between her breasts, listening to Knopfler: "The Lily of the West."

She winks at a strapping stranger across the pub.

He's headed her way now.

She smiles, shifting her long legs and arching her neck.

Come the morning, she'll make the crossing . . . start again, perhaps in Glasgow.

But now Mell smiles up at the stranger, says: "'Tis himself."

# ABOUT THE CONTRIBUTORS:

**RAY BANKS** was born in the Kingdom of Fife, but currently lives in North East England with his wife and a quartet of despicable felines. He is the creator of Leith-born Manchester P.I. Callum Innes and his debut novel, *The Big Blind*, is out now. He can be contacted through his website: http://www.thesaturdayboy.co.uk

**JAMES O'NEAL BORN** is a career law-enforcement agent whose novels are published by Putnam, including *Walking Money* and *Shock Wave*.

**KEN BRUEN** is the author of many novels, including *The Guards*, winner of the 2004 Shamus Award. His books have been published in many languages around the world. He lives in Galway, Ireland.

**REED FARREL COLEMAN** was Brooklyn born and raised. His sixth novel, *The James Deans*, received rave reviews from the *Washington Post* and *Chicago Sun-Times*. Ken Bruen has said that Coleman has the soul of an Irishman and, with this story, he hopes to prove it.

**EOIN COLFER** is a teacher from Wexford, Ireland. He spends most of his time writing about leprechauns and other magical creatures. He is best known for his fantasy series featuring criminal mastermind teenager Artemis Fowl. Eoin lived in Dublin for three years and visits whenever he needs inspiration.

**JIM FUSILLI** is the author of the award-winning Terry Orr series, which includes *Hard, Hard City*, winner of the Gumshoe Award for Best Novel of 2004, as well as *Closing Time, A Well-Known Secret*, and *Tribeca Blues*. He also writes for *The Wall Street Journal* and is a contributor to National Public Radio's *All Things Considered*.

**PATRICK J. LAMBE** lives in New Jersey, where he works as a telephone technician and writes crime stories. Third-generation Irish, English was his grandparent's second language and he hopes to one day stride the streets of Dublin, a city that lives large in his imagination as his ancestrial homeland.

**LAURA LIPPMAN** is a Baltimore writer best known for her series about Baltimore-based P.I. Tess Monaghan. She has also written two stand-alone novels, *Every Secret Thing* and *To the Power of Three*. A *Baltimore Sun* reporter for twelve years, she has written for the *New York Times*, the *Washington Post*, and Slate.com. Her work has won virtually all the major prizes given to U.S. crime writers, including the Edgar, Anthony, Agatha, Shamus, and Nero Wolfe.

**CRAIG MCDONALD** was a contributor to the 2004 *New York Times* nonfiction bestseller *Secrets of the Code*. His short stories and articles have appeared in the *Mississippi Review* and the Australia-based *Crime Factory*. Another short story won the 2005 *Philadelphia City Paper* mystery fiction contest. He is also the author of *Art in the Blood*, a collection of interviews conducted with twenty top crime fiction writers.

**PAT MULLAN** was born in Ireland and has lived in England, Canada, and the U.S.A. Formerly a banker, he now lives in Connemara, in the west of Ireland. He is the author of two novels, *The Circle of Sodom* and *Blood Red Square*. His poetry and other work appears frequently in The Dublin Writers' Workshop (www.dublinwriters.org). For more information, visit him at www.patmullan.com

**GARY PHILLIPS'S** work has been influenced by the likes of Ralph Ellison, Rod Serling, and Stan Lee. With Jervey Tervalon, he coedited the acclaimed anthology *The Cocaine Chronicles* for Akashic Books. His story in this anthology is a prequel in the life of protagonist Zelmont Raines who previously appeared in the crime novel, *The Jook*. And taking his cues from Zelmont, Phillips is busy hustling his next writing gig.

**JOHN RICKARDS** is the twenty-seven-year-old author of *Winter's End* and *The Touch of Ghosts*. He writes full-time and lives in the UK. He drinks an obscene amount of Guinness.

**PETER SPIEGELMAN** is the Shamus Award–winning author of *Black Maps* and *Death's Little Helpers*, both of which feature private investigator John March. He currently resides in Connecticut, where he is at work on another March novel.

**JASON STARR** is the author of seven noir crime novels, which are published in ten languages. His novel *Tough Luck* was an Anthony Award finalist and a Barry Award winner. He lives with his wife and daughter in New York City.

**OLEN STEINHAUER** has been nominated for numerous awards, including the Edgar and the Dagger. His most recent novel is *36 Yalta Boulevard*. He lives in Budapest.

**DUANE SWIERCZYNSKI'S** recent crime thriller *The Wheelman* features a mute Irish getaway driver named Lennon. As his last name indicates, he's not exactly Irish, but his wife and kids are. And that's good enough for him. His other books include *Secret Dead Men* and *The Big Book O' Beer*. Visit him at www.duaneswierczynski.com.

**CHARLIE STELLA** is a former "knockaround guy" who spent eighteen years working the streets of New York while trying to break into the crime fiction business. He's done everything from window cleaning (for ten years) on scaffolds high atop New York City skyscrapers to word processing to collecting for loansharks and running a bookmaking office. He's not as cute as Rocky Balboa, but he has a beautiful wife and doggie.

**SARAH WEINMAN** is the crime fiction columnist for the *Baltimore Sun* and the editor of the literary blog "Confessions of an Idiosyncratic Mind." Her work has appeared in many venues, including the *Washington Post*, the *Globe and Mail*, and the *Philadelphia City Paper*. "Hen Night" was inspired by a trip to Dublin during the 2003 Bank Holiday weekend, after which she vowed never to go back to Temple Bar.

**KEVIN WIGNALL** studied Politics & International Relations at Lancaster and is a member of Chatham House, the institute for international affairs in London. His novels include *People Die* and *For the Dogs*, and he's a regular contributor of short stories to *Ellery Queen's Mystery Magazine*. His story for this collection is, he tells us, semi-autobiographical, though he refuses to elaborate further.

# Also available from the Akashic Books Noir Series

## D.C. NOIR
edited by George Pelecanos
304 pages, a trade paperback original, $14.95

*Brand new stories by:* George Pelecanos, Laura Lippman, James Grady, Kenji Jasper, Jim Beane, Ruben Castaneda, Robert Wisdom, James Patton, Norman Kelley, Jennifer Howard, Jim Fusilli, Richard Currey, Lester Irby, Quintin Peterson, Robert Andrews, and David Slater.

GEORGE PELECANOS is a screenwriter, independent-film producer, award-winning journalist, and the author of the bestselling series of Derek Strange novels set in and around Washington, D.C., where he lives with his wife and children.

## BROOKLYN NOIR
edited by Tim McLoughlin
350 pages, a trade paperback original, $15.95
*Winner of SHAMUS AWARD, ANTHONY AWARD, ROBERT L. FISH
MEMORIAL AWARD; Finalist for EDGAR AWARD, PUSHCART PRIZE

Twenty brand new crime stories from New York's punchiest borough. Contributors include: Pete Hamill, Arthur Nersesian, Maggie Estep, Nelson George, Neal Pollack, Sidney Offit, Ken Bruen, and others.

"*Brooklyn Noir* is such a stunningly perfect combination that you can't believe you haven't read an anthology like this before. But trust me—you haven't. Story after story is a revelation, filled with the requisite sense of place, but also the perfect twists that crime stories demand. The writing is flat-out superb, filled with lines that will sing in your head for a long time to come."
—Laura Lippman, winner of the Edgar, Agatha, and Shamus awards

## BROOKLYN NOIR 2: THE CLASSICS
edited by Tim McLoughlin
309 pages, trade paperback, $15.95

*Brooklyn Noir* is back with a vengeance, this time with masters of yore mixing with the young blood: H.P. Lovecraft, Lawrence Block, Donald Westlake, Pete Hamill, Jonathan Lethem, Colson Whitehead, Irwin Shaw, Carolyn Wheat, Thomas Wolfe, Hubert Selby, Stanley Ellin, Gilbert Sorrentino, Maggie Estep, and Salvatore La Puma.

## BALTIMORE NOIR
### edited by Laura Lippman
252 pages, a trade paperback original, $14.95

*Brand new stories by:* David Simon, Laura Lippman, Tim Cockey, Rob Hiaasen, Robert Ward, Sujata Massey, Jack Bludis, Rafael Alvarez, Marcia Talley, Joseph Wallace, Lisa Respers France, Charlie Stella, Sarah Weinman, Dan Fesperman, Jim Fusilli, and Ben Neihart.

LAURA LIPPMAN has lived in Baltimore most of her life and she would have spent even more time there if the editors of the *Sun* had agreed to hire her earlier. She attended public schools and has lived in several of the city's distinctive neighborhoods, including Dickeyville, Tuscany-Canterbury, Evergreen, and South Federal Hill.

## SAN FRANCISCO NOIR
### edited by Peter Maravelis
292 pages, a trade paperback original, $14.95

*Brand new stories by:* Domenic Stansberry, Barry Gifford, Eddie Muller, Robert Mailer Anderson, Michelle Tea, Peter Plate, Kate Braverman, David Corbett, Alejandro Murguía, Sin Soracco, Alvin Lu, Jon Longhi, Will Christopher Baer, Jim Nesbit, and David Henry Sterry.

## CHICAGO NOIR
### edited by Neal Pollack
252 pages, a trade paperback original, $14.95

*Brand new stories by:* Neal Pollack, Achy Obejas, Alexai Galaviz-Budziszewski, Adam Langer, Joe Meno, Peter Orner, Kevin Guilfoile, Bayo Ojikutu, Jeff Allen, Luciano Guerriero, Claire Zulkey, Andrew Ervin, M.K. Meyers, Todd Dills, C.J. Sullivan, Daniel Buckman, Amy Sayre-Roberts, and Jim Arndorfer.